I0656951

Frederick Wedmore

Fine Prints

Frederick Wedmore

Fine Prints

ISBN/EAN: 9783337252144

Printed in Europe, USA, Canada, Australia, Japan

Cover: Foto ©Andreas Hilbeck / pixelio.de

More available books at **www.hansebooks.com**

The
Collector Series

✛ ✛ ✛

MR. GEORGE REDWAY begs to announce the publication of this series of books, each volume of which will discuss some one of the subjects which are of interest to Collectors.

Coins and Medals, Engravings, Pictures and Drawings, Postage Stamps, Book Plates, Autographs, Armour and Weapons, Plate, Porcelain and Pottery, Old Violins, Japanese Curios, and Bric-a-brac of all sorts, will be dealt with, each in a separate volume, and by a writer specially conversant with his subject. The instinct for collecting has been made the butt for much cheap ridicule by those who confound it with the mere aimless bringing together of objects which have no other merit than their rarity. But it has repeatedly been proved that skill and patience are more helpful to success in collecting than length of purse, and it is especially for those who desire to pursue their amusement with intelligent economy that this series has been planned.

The great prizes in the older forms of collecting have long since been won, and though it may be needful in these handbooks to refer occasionally to a book, a coin, a postage stamp, or a particular "state" of an etching or engraving, of which only a single example exists, the object of the series will mainly be to describe those specimens which are still attainable by the amateurs who will take the pains to hunt them down.

For this reason, though the series will be written by experts, it will be written by experts who have in view, not the visitors to the great Museums of Europe, but the amateur and collector of moderate means, who is anxious to specialise in some one or two departments of his favourite studies, and to whom it is still open by care and judgment to bring together, at a moderate expense, small yet perfect collections which any museum would be glad to possess.

Arrangements have been made with many well-known writers and specialists for their assistance as authors or editors of volumes of the series.

Each volume will contain from 250 to 300 octavo pages, from twelve to twenty plates, and a title-page designed by Mr. Laurence Housman. The series will be printed, from new type, on specially-prepared paper, by Messrs. Ballantyne, Hanson & Co.

The price of each volume of the series will be 7s. 6d. net.

The Publisher reserves the right to issue a limited number of copies of any volume of the series either on Japanese vellum, or Whatman or India paper, or with the illustrations in "proof" state, according as the subject of the book may suggest. The number of these will be announced in each case, and they will be strictly reserved for Subscribers before publication.

The Series will be published in America by Messrs. Longmans, Green & Co., Fifth Avenue, New York.

4

Collector Series

FINE PRINTS

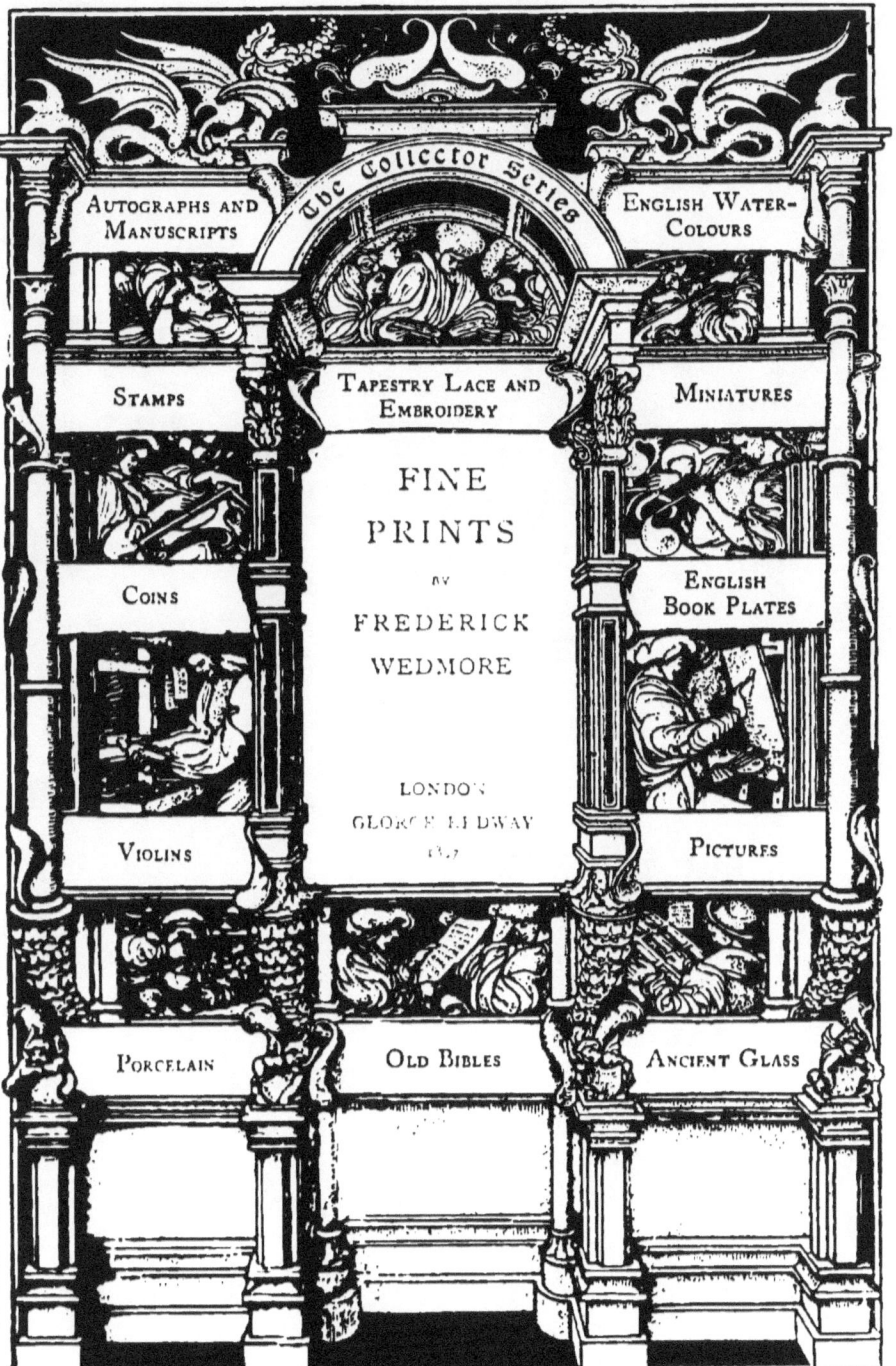

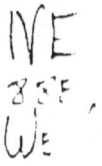

CONTENTS

ILLUSTRATIONS

FINE PRINTS

INTRODUCTION

IN the collecting of prints—of prints which must be fine and may most probably be rare—there is an ample recompense for the labour of the diligent, and room for the exercise of the most various tastes. Certain of the objects on which the modern collector sets his hands have, it may be, hardly any other virtue than the doubtful one of scarcity; but fine prints, whatever School they may belong to, and whatever may be the money value that happens to be affixed to them by the fashion of the time, have always the fascination of beauty and the interest of historical association. Then, considered as collections of works of art, there is the practical convenience of their compactness. The print-collector carries a museum in a portfolio, or packs away a picture gallery, neatly, within the compass of one solander-box.

Again, the print-collector, if he will but occupy himself with intelligent industry, may, even to-day, have a collection of fine things without paying overmuch, or even very much, for them. All will depend upon the School or master that he particularly affects. Has he at his disposal only a few bank-notes, or only a few sovereigns even, every year?—he may yet surround himself with excellent possessions, of which he will not speedily exhaust the charm. Has he the fortune of an Astor or a Vanderbilt?—he may instruct the greatest dealers in the trade to struggle in the auction-room, on his behalf, with the representatives of the Berlin Museum. And it may be his triumph, then, to have paid the princely ransom of the very rarest "state" of the rarest Rembrandt. And, all the time, whether he be rich man or poor—but especially, I think, if he be poor—he will have been educating himself to the finer perception of a masculine yet lovely art, and, over and above indulging the "fad" of the collector, he will find that his possessions rouse within him an especial interest in some period of Art History, teach him a real and delicate discrimination of an artist's qualities, and so, indeed, enlarge his vista that his enjoyment of life itself, and his appreciation of it, is quickened and sustained. For great Art of any kind, whether it be the painter's, the engraver's, the sculptor's, or the writer's, is not—it cannot be too often insisted—a mere craft or sleight-of-hand, to be practised from the wrist downwards. It is the expression of the man himself. It is, therefore, with great and new personalities that the study of an art, the contemplation of it—not the mere bungling amateur performance of it—brings you into contact. And there is no way of studying an art that is so complete and satisfactory as the collecting of examples of it.

And then again, to go back to the material part of

10

the business, how economical it is to be a collector, if only you are wise and prudent! Of pleasant vices this is surely the least costly. Nay, more; the bank-note cast upon the waters may come back after many days.

The study of engravings, ancient and modern—of woodcuts, line engravings, etchings, mezzotints—has become by this time extremely elaborate and immensely complicated. Most people know nothing of it, and do not even realise that behind all their ignorance there is a world of learning and of pleasure, some part of which at least might be theirs if they would but enter on the land and seek to possess it. Few men, even of those who address themselves to the task, acquire swiftly any substantial knowledge of more than one or two departments of the study; though the ideal collector, and I would even say the reasonable one, whatever he may actually own, is able, sooner or later, to take a survey of the larger ground—his eye may range intelligently over fields he has no thought of annexing.

From this it will be concluded—and concluded rightly—that the print-collector must be a specialist, more or less. More or less, at least at the beginning, must he address himself with particular care to one branch of the study. And which is it to be? The number of fine Schools of Etching and Engraving is really so considerable that the choice may well be his own. This or that master, this or that period, this or that method, he may select with freedom, and will scarcely go wrong. But the mention of it brings one, naturally, to the divisions of the subject, and the

11

collector, we shall find, is face to face, first of all, with this question : " Are the prints I am to bring together to be the work of an artist who originates, or of an artist who mainly translates ? "

Well, of course, in a discussion of the matter, the great original Schools must have the first place, whatever it may be eventually decided shall be the subject of your collection. You may buy, by all means, the noble mezzotints which the engravers of the Eighteenth Century wrought after Reynolds, Romney, and George Morland ; but suffer us to say a little first about the great creative artists, and then, when the possible collector has read about them—and has made himself familiar, at the British Museum Print-room say, with some portion of their work—it may be that though he finds that they are nearly all, however different in themselves, less decorative on a wall than the great masters of rich mezzotint, he will find a charm and spell he cannot wish to banish in the evidence of their originality, in the fact that they are the creations of an individual impulse, whether they are slight or whether they are elaborate.

The Schools of early line-engravers, Italian, Flemish, German, are almost entirely Schools of original production. I say "almost," for as early as the days of Raphael, the interpreter, the translator, the copyist, if you will, came into the matter, and the designs of the Urbinate were multiplied by the burin of Marc Antonio and his followers. And charming prints they are, these Marc Antonios, so little bought to-day. Economical of line they are, and exquisite of contour, and likely, one would suppose, to be valued in the Future more than they are valued just now, when the rhyme of Mr. Browning, about the collector of his early period, is true no longer—

> " The debt of wonder my crony owes
> Is paid to my Marc Antonios."

That in the main the earlier work is original, is not a thing to be surprised at, any more than it is a thing to lament. The narrow world of buyers in that primitive day was not likely to afford scope for the business of the translator ; the time had not yet come when there was any need for the creations of an artist to be largely multiplied. That time came first, perhaps, in the Seventeenth Century, when the immediately accepted genius of Rubens gave ground for the employment of the interpreting talent of Bolswert, Pontius, and Vosterman. Again, there was Edelinck, Nanteuil, and the Drevets.

It need scarcely be said that extreme rarity is a characteristic of the early Schools. The prints of two of the most masculine of the Italians, for instance, Andrea Mantegna and Jacopo de' Barbarj, are not to be got by ordering them. They have, of course, to be watched for, and waited for, and the opportunity taken at the moment at which it arises. In some measure there will be experienced the same engaging and preventive difficulty in possessing yourself of the prints of the great Germans and of the one great Flemish master,

Lucas of Leyden. And if these, in certain states at least, in certain conditions, are not quite as hard to come upon as the works of those masters who have been mentioned just before them, and of their compatriots of the same period, that is but an extra inducement for the search, since there is, of course, a degree of difficulty that is actually discouraging—a sensible man does not long aim at the practically impossible. Now in regard to the early Flemish master with whom Dürer himself not unwillingly—nay, very graciously—exchanged productions, there are yet no insuperable obstacles to the collector gathering together a representative array of his work; it is possible upon occasion even to add one or two of his scarce and beautiful and spirited ornaments to the group, such as it may be, of subjects based on scriptural or on classic themes. To be a specialist in Lucas van Leyden would be to be unusual, but not perhaps to be unwise; yet a greater sagacity would, no doubt, be manifested by concentration upon that which is upon the whole the finer work of Albert Dürer. Of late years, Martin Schöngauer too, with the delicacy of his burin, his tenderness of sentiment, and his scarcely less pronounced quaintness, has been a favourite, greatly sought for; but, amongst the Germans, the work that best upon the whole repays the trouble undertaken in amassing it, is that of the great Albert himself, and that of the best of the Little Masters.

And who then were the Little Masters? a beginner wants to know. They were seven artists, some of them Dürer's direct pupils, all of them his direct successors;.

14

INTRODUCTION

getting the name that is common to them not from any insignificance in their themes, but from the scale on which it pleased them to execute their always deliberate, always highly-wrought work. There is not one who has not about his labour some measure of individual interest, but the three greatest of the seven are the two brothers Beham—Barthel and Sebald—and that Prince of little ornamentists, Heinrich Aldegrever. Nowhere was the German Renaissance greater than in its ornament, and the Behams, along with subjects of Allegory, History, and Genre, addressed themselves not seldom to subjects of pure and self-contained design. Rich and fine in their fancy, their characteristic yet not too obvious symmetry has an attraction that lasts. Barthel was the less prolific of the twain, but perhaps the more vigorous in invention. Sebald, certainly not at a loss himself for motives for design, yet chose to fall back on occasion—as in the exquisite little print of the *Adam and Eve*—upon the inventions of his brother. There is not now, there never has been, very much collecting here in England of the German Little Masters. Three pounds or four suffices, now and again, to buy at Sotheby's, or at a dealer's, a good Beham, a good Aldegrever. In their own land they are rated a little more highly—are at least more eagerly sought for—but with research and pains (and remembering resolutely in this, as in every other case, to reject a bad impression), it is possible, for a most moderate sum, to have quite a substantial bevy of these treasures; and though large indeed in their design, their real art quality, they

are, in a material sense, as small almost as gems. Mr.
Loftie, who made .. specialty of Sebald Behams, was
able, I believe, to carry a collection of them safely
housed in his waistcoat-pocket.

If we pass on from the Sixteenth to the Seventeenth
Century, we have the opportunity, if we so choose, of
leaving Line Engraving, and of studying and acquiring
here and there examples of the noblest Etching that
has been done in the world. For the Seventeenth
Century is the period of Rembrandt—the period, too, of
that meaner but yet most skilful craftsman, Adrian van
Ostade, and the period of the serene artist of classic
Landscape and Architecture, who wrought some twenty
plates in aquafortis—I mean Claude. In an introductory chapter to a volume like the present, there is time
and space to consider only Rembrandt. And it cannot
be asserted too decisively that in the study and collection of Rembrandt, lies, as a rule—and must, one thinks,
for ever lie—the print-collector's highest and most legitimate pleasure. And even a poor man may have a few
good Rembrandts, though only quite a rich man can
have them in great numbers and of the rarest. Rembrandt is a superb tonic for people who have courted too
much the infection of a weakly and a morbid art. Not
occupied indeed in his representations of humanity with
visions of formal beauty, his variety is unsurpassed, his
vigour unequalled ; he has the great traditions of Style,
yet is as modern and as unconventional as Mr. Whistler.
Of the different classes of Rembrandt's compositions,
the sacred subjects perhaps — at least some minor

examples of them—are the least uncommon ; and in their intimate and homely study of humanity, and often too in their *technique*, the sacred subjects prove themselves desirable. Never, however, should they be collected to the exclusion of the rarer Portraiture or of the rarest Landscape. A *Lutma*, a *De Jonghe*, in a fine state and fine condition, a *Cottage with a Dutch Hay-barn*, a *Landscape with a Tower*, attain the summit of the etcher's art, and, both in noble conception and magical execution, are absolutely perfect. Why, such impressions of the Rembrandt landscapes as were dispersed but two or three years since, when the cabinet of Mr. Holford passed under the hammer, appeal to the trained eye with a potency not a whit less great than can any masterpiece of Painting ; and, to speak in very soberest English, no sum of money that it could ever enter into the heart of the enthusiast to pay for them would be, in truth, a too extravagant, a too unreasonable ransom.

In the Eighteenth Century original Etching falls into the background, and the skill of the engraver, in those lands where, in the Eighteenth Century, it was chiefly exercised—in France, that is, and England—is devoted in the main to no spontaneous creation, but to the translation of the work of painters. In two mediums, thoroughly opposed or thoroughly contrasted, yet each with its own value, the engraver's labour is executed ; there flourished, side by side, the delicate School of Line Engraving and the noble School of Mezzotint. Reproductive or interpretive Line Engraving had done great

17   B

things a generation or so earlier, and even Mezzotint
was not the invention of the Eighteenth Century, though
it was then that the art discovered by Von Siegen, and
practised with a singular directness by Prince Rupert, was
brought to its perfection. But the Eighteenth Century
—even the latter half of it—was certainly the period
at which both arts were busiest; and not so much the
professed collector as the intelligent *bourgeois* of the
time gathered these things together—in England chiefly
Mezzotints, in France chiefly Line Engravings—and a
very few shillings paid for the M'Ardell or the Watson
after Reynolds, and later for the Raphael Smith or
the William Ward after George Morland. Often the
engraver was a publisher of his own and other people's
prints. That was the case in Paris as much as in
London; and in Paris, in the third quarter of the
Eighteenth Century, the line engravers issued for a
couple of francs or so—and the *Mercure de France* was
apt, like newspapers in our own day, to notice the
publication—those admirable, and still in England, too
little known prints which record the dignified observation, the sober, just suggested comedy of Chardin.

There were exceptions, of course, to the common rule
that in the period of our first Georges, and of Louis the
Fifteenth, engraver's work was translation. Hogarth,
in the first half of the century—about the time when
the French line engravers were occupied with their
quite exquisite translations of the grace of Watteau,
Lancret, and Pater—wrought out on copper with
rough vigour his original conceptions of the Rake's

18

and of the Harlot's *Progress*, and not a few of his
minor themes ; but when it came to the rendering into
black and white of those masterly canvases of *Marriage
à la Mode*, professional engravers, such as Ravenet and
Scotin, were employed to admirable purpose, and a
little later the very colours of the canvas seemed to
live, the painter's very touch seemed to be reproduced,
in the noble mezzotints of Earlom. And the immense
successes of this reproductive engraving, with the art of
Hogarth, brings us back to the truth of our earlier pro-
position ; the period was a period of interpretation, not
of original work, with the engraver. The whole French
Eighteenth Century School, from Watteau down to
Lavreince, is to be studied, and collected, too, in Line
Engraving. The School is not invariably discreet in
subject : Lavreince has his suggestiveness, though rarely
does he go beyond legitimate comedy, and Baudouin,
François Boucher's son-in-law, has his audacities ; but
against these is to be set the dignified idyl of the great
master of Valenciennes ; the work of Watteau's pupils,
too ; the works of Boucher ; Massard's consummate
rendering, in finest or most finished line, of this or
that seductive vision of Greuze ; the stately comedy
of Moreau le Jeune ; and, as I have said already, the
excellent interpretations of the homely, natural, so
desirable art of Chardin.

Mezzotint really did for all the English painters of
importance of the Eighteenth Century, and in a measure
for certain earlier Dutchmen, all that Line Engraving
accomplished for the French. " By these men I shall

be immortalised," Sir Joshua said, when the work of M'Ardell and his fellows came under his view. Gainsborough, it is true, was not interpreted quite so much or quite so successfully. But Romney has as much justice done to him in later English Mezzotint as the luxurious art of Lely and Kneller obtained from one of the earlier practitioners of the craft—John Smith. Morland's continued and justified popularity in our own time is due to nothing half as much as to the mezzotints by Raphael Smith, and Ward, and Young, and others of that troop of brethren. And it was mezzotint, in combination with the bitten line for leading features of the composition, that Turner, early in our own century—in 1807—decided to employ in the production of those seventy plates of *Liber Studiorum* upon which, already even, so much of his fame rests.

Liber Studiorum occupies an interesting and a peculiar position between work upon the copper wholly original and work wholly reproductive. Turner etched the leading lines himself. In several cases he completed, with his own hand, in mezzotint, the whole of the engraved picture; but generally he gave the "scraping" to a professional engraver, whose efforts he minutely supervised and most elaborately corrected. In recent years, almost as much, though not quite as much sought for as the *Liber* plates of Turner, are certain rather smaller mezzotints which record the art of Constable; but Constable himself did nothing on these plates, though he supervised their production by David Lucas. Turner's connection with professional engravers was not confined to the priceless and admirable prints of the *Liber*. He trained a school of line engravers, welcoming at first the assistance of John Pye and of George and William Cooke. These two brothers were the engravers mainly of his *Southern Coast*, and nothing has been more manly than that; but the work of William Miller, in the *Clovelly* of that *Southern Coast*, and in a subsequent series, interpreted with quite peculiar exquisiteness those refinements of light which in Turner's middle and later time so much engaged his effort.

With Turner's death, or with the death of the artists who translated him, fine Line Engraving almost vanished. It had all but disappeared when, nearly fifty years ago, there began in France and England that Revival of Etching with which the amateur of to-day is so rightly concerned. A few etchings by Bracquemond—of still-life chiefly—a larger number by Jules Jacquemart, of fine objects in porcelain, jewellery, bronze, and noble stones, are amongst the more precious products of the earlier part of the Revival of Etching, and they are so treated that they are inventions indeed, and of an originality that is exquisite. But the greatest event of the earlier years of the Revival was the appearance, as long ago as 1850, of the genius of Méryon, who, during but a few years, wrought a series of *chefs-d'œuvre*—inspired visions of Paris—and died, neglected and ignored, in the great city to which it is he who has raised, in those few prints of his, the noblest of all monuments.

Two other men of very different genius and of unsurpassed energy we associate with this revival of Etching. Both are yet with us in the fulness of their years; and both will occupy the collector who is wise in his generation, and will be, one may make bold to say, the delight of the far Future as well as of the Present. I mean Sir Seymour Haden and Mr. James Whistler. The prints of Seymour Haden shame no cabinet; the best of Whistler's scarcely suffer at all when placed beside the master-work of Rembrandt. But it is dangerous treating much of contemporaries when one's task is chiefly with the dead; and though I might mention many other not unworthy men, of whom some subsequent historian must take count— nay, who may even be referred to at a later stage of this volume—I will confine myself here, in this introductory chapter, to just the intimation that Legros and Helleu are, next after the etchers I have already named, those probably who should engage attention.

CHAPTER I

A LITTLE Guide to Print Collecting such as the present one, even if written on very personal lines, not in the least concealing the writer's own prepossessions, and giving therefore, quite possibly, what may seem disproportionate notice of certain masters, cannot, of course, hope to entirely suffice for the special student of any particular man. The special student will not, if he is reasonable, find that the little book falls short of its aim, and fails to do its proper work, because it does not and cannot possibly supply within its limited volume all the information of which the accomplished student is himself possessed, and which he feels to be more or less indispensable even to the beginner who desires to be thorough. He will know—and will scarcely need that I should here remind him—that not one book, nor even a hundred books, can make an expert, can turn the tyro into a practical connoisseur. What the tyro wants is experience, all that is learnt by loss and gain, and by brushing shoulder to shoulder with dealers and brother-collectors and the auctioneer in the auction-room. He wants that, to become a practical collector at all, and to become a specialist he wants that and something more. He wants access to and acquaintance with a large and considerable branch of what is now unquestionably an immense literature. There are larger books than this of mine on the general theme of Print Collecting, and they have been written at different times, with different prepossessions, with different prejudices, from different points of view. But over and above these larger books there is a library of monographs on particular masters, works which are nearly always *Catalogues raisonnés*, and often treatises to boot; and while no one of these monographs can be altogether neglected by the would-be student of the artist with whom it is concerned, some of them must be among the most cherished of his companions, among the voiceless but instructive friends whose society is education. No little book then, like the present one, can take the place of experience and of the study of many books; and least of all perhaps can a book which does not affect to be the abstract and brief chronicle of what has been done before, but which prefers rather to approach its large subject from the point of view of an individual collector, who yet, it must be said, while cultivating specialties, has not been inaccessible to the charm of much that lies beyond the limits of any fields of his own.

24

THE TASK OF THE COLLECTOR

So much by way of explanation—by way, too, of disarming the kind of criticism which would judge a general endeavour only by the success with which it seemed to meet the needs of a particular case. A Bibliography of the subject, which will be found on later pages, and which must itself be a selection, comparatively brief, from the mass of material that bears upon the theme, will suffice to set the student of the special school or master upon the desirable track ; and meanwhile one thing may be done, nor, as I hope, that one thing only : the would-be tiller of the particular plot may be reminded of the vastness of the land. Even of print collecting it is true, sometimes, that the trees prevent you from seeing the forest.

I have said just now, in the print-collector's world, how vast is the land ! Time, of course, tends to extend it—would extend it inevitably, by reason of new production, did not Fashion sometimes intervene, and, while opening to the explorer some new tract, taboo a district over which he had aforetime been accustomed to wander. The fashions of the wise are not wholly without reason, but the fashions of the foolish have also to be reckoned with. As an instance, the very generation that has seen the most just appraisement of original Etching has witnessed too the exaltation of Bartolozzi and of his nerveless School, a decline of interest in Marc Antonio, even to some extent in Albert Dürer, and a silly rage for the coloured print which fifty years since was the appropriate ornament of scrapbook and nursery.

I have spoken harshly of two classes of things which within the last few years have found eager purchasers, and it is incumbent upon me that I justify my harshness and warn the beginner all the more effectually thereby. The Bartolozzis, then, which have been puffed so absurdly—what is their real place? To begin with, they are—and in this one respect they resemble Marc Antonios indeed, and the justly extolled mezzotints which translate Sir Joshua—they are the work of an engraver who interpreted the theme of another, and not of an engraver who invented his own. But this it is evident that they may be, and yet by no means be criminal. Wherein, it may be asked fairly, lies their greater offence? It lies in this. That the Humanity they depict is generally without character —that in no austere and in no captivating, overwhelming beauty, but in its feeble grace, lies its chief virtue. Bartolozzi was a good draughtsman. He was no doubt correct habitually, and he was habitually elegant. Academic he was, though competent. But again, how terribly monotonous was the order of his beauty, and how weakly sentimental the design of those—Cipriani and Angelica Kaufmann principal amongst them—to whose conceptions he lent at least a measure of support! Of Bartolozzi's works, the best for the collector are the "Tickets." They are on a small scale — dainty little engraved invitations or announcements to the public of their day, giving the opportunity to hear Giardini or Madame Banti, or some other singer of songs or maker of excellent music.

26

Delightful little compositions they undoubtedly are, with the nude drawn charmingly. Half-a-dozen of them I would possess with satisfaction. But all the rest!—all those Bartolozzis which, as they increase in size, get (just as photographs do) increasingly meaningless! The reasonable collector, if his instinct be fine or his taste educated, will not desire these, even at prices that may be comparatively insignificant, whilst Rembrandts, Dürers, Hogarths, Watteaus, Méryons, Whistlers, exist to delight the world.

The coloured print—for it is time to make some brief allusion to it—is often very "taking." To the novice who does not think, it may even appear to be entirely desirable. But, like the average Bartolozzi, it is trivial at best. A pretty enough decoration for the wall of a room in which artistic taste is neither accomplished nor severe, it has at least to be recognised that its art is hybrid. The weight and value of the light and shade of the engraving are apt to be minimised or discounted by the application of colour; and the colour, though put on with ingenuity, has little of the gradation and the subtle blending, and nothing whatever of the " touch," in which the art of the painter in some measure consists. That is why a set of Wheatley's "Cries of London," printed in bistre, is far better than a set which has the superficial gaiety of many hues. A coloured Morland is a Morland murdered. More tolerant may we be of the coloured prints of France; the lighter art of a Taunay or of a Debucourt according not so ill with the application of a process which boasts no other charm

than the charm of the *à peu près*. But even where the
coloured print is least offensive or least inadequate, no
one can affect to discover in it the more serious qualities
of Art. Often, experts inform us, the colour was only
applied when the original work upon the plate was
half worn out—when the plate could yield no longer an
impression that was satisfactory. Then it was, at least
in some cases, that the aid of colour—or some approxi-
mation to the colour that a painter might have sought
to realise—was called in, and so the opportunity prepared for the foolish rich of our period to pay great
prices for an engaging *pis-aller*.

Uninstructed acquaintances, ill-judging dealers, and
the habit of an indolent world to regard old prints as
humble examples of decorative furniture—all these com-
bine to make it possible for the beginner, and even for
the man of many winters who is outside Art, to spend
his time in accumulating objects no one of which is of
the first order. Even certain print-sellers, who ought
to do much better, but who possess, we must suppose,
more of technical knowledge than of sure and well-
established taste, lend themselves to the diffusion of
the love of the second-rate. There are several high-
class dealers now in London, people of probity and of
accomplishment, some of them young men, too—a circumstance which bodes well for the future. But those
were safer days when the world of the collector lay
within narrower limits, and when the close contact that
there was wont to be between a few learned salesmen
and a few scarcely less learned purchasers, who bought,

of course, gradually, who never bought things *en bloc*—
who studied and enjoyed, in fine, instead of merely
possessed—made it an unlikely matter that any quarter
would be shown to the unworthy productions of a
vague and indifferent art. But the beginner of to-day
must take things as he finds them. If the root of the
matter be in him, his mistakes need not be serious.
The opportunities for sagacious choice in collecting yet
remain frequent. If he collects fine things, he will not,
of course, succeed in acquiring so extensive a cabinet as
that which rejoiced the heart of his forerunner when
prices were much lower—when a Rembrandt, now worth
a hundred guineas, was sold for a ten-pound note. He
must recognise, too, that a very large number of the
finest impressions—and it is upon fine impressions only
that his mind should be set—have come to be cloistered
in National, in University, even in some cases in Municipal institutions. But yet the field that is open to
him is a wide one, and, as was said in the Introduction,
it is possible for diligence and intelligence to accomplish
much, even if unaccompanied by a purse that is big
and deep.

It has been customary in books on Collecting to say
something about the qualities that are desirable in a
print—the qualities, I mean, that, in their combination
constitute, not a fine subject—that is a different matter
altogether—but a fine impression, an impression such
as the collector should wish to possess. And though,
no doubt, for certain readers, the treatise of Maberly,
and the later and ampler treatise of Dr. Willshire,

may be without difficulty accessible, the expert will hold me blameless for not forgetting here the interests of the beginner, and for therefore going, though it shall be rapidly, over ground that, to the connoisseur, must needs be familiar.

The first and most indispensable requisite, then, for a fine impression of a print, ancient or modern, is that the plate betray no signs of wear, so that the scheme of the artist in line and light and shade shall be presented still with virgin intactness. It may be a high ideal to aim at, but it is not unattainable; and practically it is as necessary in a Dürer three hundred years old as in a Whistler which may have been wrought only twelve years ago. Very different qualities of surface are, of course, sought for in prints of different kinds, devoted to different effects. The perfection of one plate may be attained when it is "brilliant;" the perfection of another when it is "rich." But in all, the signs of wear, and, in nearly all, the signs of re-touching, are to be avoided. Wear is indicated perhaps most easily by the absence of clearness in lines designed to be distinct, and by an acquired evenness and monotony in passages which obviously were never meant to be monotonous and even. Re-touching is a more subtle matter. It is generally resorted to to repair the wear; and sometimes the re-touching is the work of the original artist, and sometimes it is the work of a later craftsman, concerned in the interests of publisher or dealer, or it may be in his own, if it is he who has become the possessor of the plate.

But an impression originally rich or brilliant, or brilliant and rich at once, may, by ill-usage, or even by the absence of a delicate care, have lost the qualities that commended it to its first possessor. The beginner in print collecting must assure himself not only that the work is still good, but that the surface is clean and fair. Then he must look at the back of the print, must assure himself, by careful examination there, that it has not been "backed," or patched, or mended: at all events, that all the mending it has required has been slight and neatly executed. Damp is a deadly enemy of prints. They pine for dry warm air as much as a soldier sent from out of Provence into the chilliness of French Flanders. "*Il parait que ça grelottait là-bas*," said a Provençal once to me at Cannes. Many a print is as sensitive to dampish cold as an American consumptive. The collector then must diagnose well—must satisfy himself as far as possible that the seeds of disease are not in the print already—and if he buys the print, he must see to its health carefully.

Let me here hasten, though, to assure him nothing more than reasonable care is required, and I will tell him at once in what it consists. If he frames his print, he had better order that the thickness of some moderate mount—an eighth or twelfth of an inch is fully enough for the purpose—intervenes between the surface of the print and the glass. The glass may "sweat" from time to time, and obviously its moisture must not be deposited upon the very object it exists to guard. If a print has great money value, or if from any cause the collector sets much store by it, it should not remain in any frame for more than a few years without at least a careful re-examination. Fresh air will do it good; and, moreover, it is good for the collector's own eye (whose delicacy ought to be culti-vated by all possible means) that account be taken of a print's appearance not only when it is under glass. If the collector, instead of framing his print, puts it in a portfolio, he must see at least that it is so handled and managed that its surface is not rubbed by the backs of other prints, or the backs of their mounts. Where one print follows another in a portfolio or solander-box, the mounts of all should be smooth. The portfolio must keep dust out as well as it can. The solander-box will keep dust out much better. And whether the print is in folio or box, or laid naked in the drawer or shelf of a cabinet, it should be from time to time looked at, given, so to put it, a " bath of air " on a sunny and dry day. A country-house, unless the walls are very thick and the rooms kept very carefully, is not the best place for a collection of prints, which (in England at least) flourish most in the atmosphere of cities. It is in cities that they require the least solici-tude. I know very well, when I say this, that it will be news to some people that prints require any solicitude at all. I have pointed out that they do, but also that their possession does not involve any overwhelming responsibility.

There is one other point as to the condition of a print—as to that which it is desirable to find in it before we purchase it—that should be touched upon before this chapter ends. That is the question of margin. It may be that some worthy people are almost as sharply divided upon the question of margin as are New York *gourmets* upon the question of how many minutes it takes to roast to perfection a canvas-back duck. But the majority of collectors are advocates of margins: they "take curious pleasure" in them, Mr. Whistler remarks. A margin undoubtedly has much to recommend it. While a print is mounted, and even after it is mounted—on those occasions, I mean, when, under examination, it passes from hand to hand—the margin helps to protect it. Yet it is evident that a margin has no artistic merit, and that therefore to establish a very great difference in money value between the print with a margin and the print with none, is to be rather absurd. Of course a print three hundred years old, which has conserved its margin to some extent, is a yet greater rarity than a print which has not; and as rarity—rarity of condition even—is paid for as well as beauty, there is some just market-value in margin, no doubt.

But, unlike that fine condition of surface on which I have so much insisted, the possession of margin is by no means strictly necessary. It is sometimes an added grace, but never, at least in the case of a print that is ancient, and that has been subjected probably to many vicissitudes—never in such a case is it an indispensable virtue. Rarely does the ample margin go back beyond the Eighteenth Century. In your etching by Méryon or

Haden—done fifty or thirty years ago—you may expect some margin, fairly. In your noble line-engraving after Chardin or Watteau, you may be glad of some, and may be grateful and surprised if you find much. In your Rembrandt, a little enhances the value. In your Dürer, an eighth of an inch, how precious and how rare !

In regard to the loss of a margin, while in the case of a very old print it is due probably to gradual ravages and various little accidents, in the case of engravings less old, and especially in the case of engravings which (mezzotints, for example) have always been held most decorative on a wall, it is due simply to the process of framing. When the mezzotint—or whatever it is—was prepared for the frame, the knife removed the margin at a stroke, and with it there perished, for the future collector, some chance of exultation and not inhuman boasting.

CHAPTER II

As I think that, speaking generally, the wisest collector
is the collector who devotes himself to original work,
we will begin the study of some various departments of
the collector's pursuit by a group of chapters on work
that is wholly original. And among work that is
wholly original, what is there that—since chronological
order cannot require to be strictly observed—deserves
to take precedence of the art of Etching? Not only is
the art up to a certain point popular to-day—that is
a consideration which need not affect the wise collector
very much—but it is, of all the arts of Black and White,
the one which lends itself most readily to the expression of a mood—therefore to the expression of a
personality. In Line-Engraving, of which the finest
examples cannot, on many grounds, be esteemed too
highly, the *chef-d'œuvre* is slow of accomplishment.

In Etching, the hour may produce the masterpiece, though indeed many a masterpiece has involved something more than the labour of a day.

Of old-world etchers whose plates should occupy the collector seriously—of old-world etchers between whom he may take his choice, or, if he prefer it, divide his attention—there are, after all, but a few. To have named Claude, Vandyke, Rembrandt, Ostade, and Hollar, is to have named the chief. Other Dutch *genre* painters than Ostade of course etched cleverly, but none with his perfection—his perfection, I mean, when he was at his best. And behind Rembrandt was a group of men, some of whom simply imitated, others of whom followed in ways more nearly their own. Other Dutchmen, again, like Backhuysen and Adrian Van de Velde and Zeeman—whom, nearly two centuries afterwards, Méryon worshipped — did work that need not be put aside. Latterly it has not been put aside; for in a recent *Portfolio* Mr. Binyon made it the subject of special study. But still the greater men are the few who were named first.

Of these great men, it was Claude, Vandyke, and Ostade who wrought the fewest plates. As for Vandyke, not only was his work not vast in quantity—his labour upon each particular plate stopped at an early stage. To the copper's detriment, as many think, others continued it, and Vandyke's etchings are only entirely his own in that first State which is the stage of the sketch. Yet are they far indeed from being

36

worthless afterwards. A background is added. The
record of character remains pretty much the same.

It was not quite thus with Claude. He, like other
great masters, and like some small ones, suffers by the
mischief of "re-touching;" but nothing done upon
his plates, or upon any imitations of them, carries the
work much further than Claude himself had carried it.
With all the free and easy handling of the point, there
is an obvious completeness—a completeness not only for
the initiated—in some of the very best of his work. In
tone, in delicacy of chiaroscuro, the plate of the *Bouvier*
—the masterpiece for atmospheric effect—is carried
as far as it could have been carried by line-engraving. It has indeed quite as much atmosphere, though
not quite as much delicacy of contour, as the marvellous
plates done on about the same scale by the translators
of Turner, whom Turner in a measure trained—I mean
especially the men who wrought upon the *Southern
Coast* series: George Cooke with *Margate*, Horsburgh
with *Whitstable*, the incomparable William Miller with
Portsmouth and *Clovelly*. Claude's *Campo Vaccino*,
again, is equally finished to the corners; and so, of
course, in its perhaps subtler fashion, is the famous
Sunset (Dumesnil, No. 15). *Cattle Going Home in
Stormy Weather* has the appearance of more summary
labour, a freedom more convincing, and more appropriate to that effect of atmosphere, which, together with
the movement of beasts and herdsmen, the plate is devoted to recording. Again, complete tonality is not
sought for—at all events is not obtained—in *Shepherd*

and Shepherdess Conversing, which yet, in the rare
First State of it, which alone is entirely worthy, is full
from end to end of Claude's happiest and freest, and—
dare one say?—most playful work in the draughtsmanship of foliage. In the Second State one tall tree is
deprived of its height and grace. The picture is spoilt;
or, if not spoilt, marred.

It is now four-and-twenty years since, at the Burlington Fine Arts Club, there was held a well-chosen and
perhaps the first and last important exhibition of the
etchings of Claude. Dumesnil's list of all Claude's work
in *aquafortis* includes forty-two prints—some of them
unimportant; and of the forty-two, the Burlington
Club, with access to the best collections everywhere
(whatever modest things may have been said on this
occasion to the contrary), managed to show twenty-six.
Besides the plates mentioned in the preceding paragraph, the *Dance by the Waterside*, the *Dance under
the Trees*, and the *Wooden Bridge* are amongst the
things one would covet. In the *Wooden Bridge* there
is the whole spirit of the broad Italian land. A fine
Second State, from the cabinet of some good collector—
my own is from John Barnard's—represents the plate
perfectly. Of the *Bouvier* you are lucky if you can get
a Second State. Sir Seymour Haden, who would never
tolerate a bad impression, long contented himself with
a Third, though some years before he parted with his
things he managed to acquire a First. That delightful
collector, Richard Fisher, had a First State of the
Cattle Going Home in Stormy Weather, and a noble

38

little print it was. Mr. Julian Marshall, who bought rare things in his youth, and keenly appreciates them (though, while in his youth still, he sold many), had, and doubtless retains, a First State of the *Rape of Europa*, which, in an impression like his own—"early, undescribed, before the plate was cleaned," says the Burlington Club Catalogue—is indeed most desirable.

As to the money value of Claude's etchings, in the "States" and the conditions in which they are alone desirable, the prices that were reached at the Seymour Haden sale in 1891 are as good an indication as one can well obtain. Sir Seymour's beautiful and silvery First State of *Le Bouvier* was knocked down at £42; his *Dance under the Trees*—a First State too—at £10; his *Sunrise* (but it was a Fourth State) at £5, 12s. 6d.; his *Shepherd and Shepherdess Conversing*, in the First State, at £7 (and this was cheap); his *Campo Vaccino*, in the First State, at £6, 6s. He had no *Wooden Bridge*. At Richard Fisher's sale, in 1892, the *Bouvier*, in a Second or Third State, fetched £15, and a good impression of the *Dance under the Trees*, £12. It will be seen that, rare though Claude's etchings are, in good condition, they do not, in England at least, when they appear in the auction-room, command prices that can be called excessive.

The etchings of Vandyke, at all events the best of them, have fetched more. It must be that their rarity, in the most desired condition, is even greater. Sir Seymour Haden had a few superb ones. Vandyke's own portrait (Dutuit, No. 3) sold in the Haden sale for £60; the pure etching of the *Snyders* for £44; the *Sutter-mans* for £30; the *Lucas Vosterman*, £50; the masterly *De Wael*—which, even in an early, well-chosen impression of a later State, one finds an enviable possession—£17, 10s. The touch of Vandyke has nothing that is comparable with Rembrandt's subtlety, yet is it decisive and immediate, and so far excellent. And Vandyke, however inclined he may have been to undue elegance—an elegance *trop voulue*—in certain painted portraits, seized firmly and nobly in his etched portraits of men (and practically his etchings are only portraits of men) the masculine character and the marked individuality of his models.

Of the etchings of Adrian van Ostade, Mr. Fisher had what was practically a complete collection—he had fifty plates; and as he was a great admirer of this unquestioned master of *technique*, this penetrating even if pessimistic observer of Life, he had taken care to have impressions of good character: in some cases, as good as it is ever possible to get. Inequality of course there was; and whilst here and there an indifferent impression fell for a few shillings, sums as important as have been paid for Ostades were realised for the rarest and the best chosen things. We will consider the prices of the most desirable. For a First State of the *Man and Woman Conversing*, £13 was the ransom. £14 was paid for even the Fourth State of that rarity, *The Empty Pitcher*. Herr Meder gave £63 for the Second State of a piece which some call spirited and some call savage, *The Quarrel with Drawn Knives*, and £26, 10s. for the First State of *A Woman Sitting on a Doorstep*. £80 was paid by the same buyer for the First State of the *Woman Singing*, and Mr. Gutekunst gave £37 for a Fourth State of *The Painter*. Could I become the owner of two masterpieces of Ostade, the pieces which I should think worthy to be dignified with that name, and which I should consequently proceed to possess, would be *The Family* and the *Peasant Paying his Reckoning*. The first — not less excellent than any other in *technique* — is full of homely piety and truth to common things. It is one of Ostade's larger pieces; and at the Fisher sale, the First State, which had been in the Hawkins collection, passed into the hands of Mr. Deprez for £23. The *Peasant Paying his Reckoning* is one of the smaller plates. As the title goes far to imply, it represents a tavern visitor making ready to leave the cosy interior; the landlady looking out with keenness for the sum that is due. The piece teems with delicate observation, not only of character, but of picturesque detail, and with light and airy touch. It was a wonderful Fourth State that was in the Fisher collection; and £42 was the price that Herr Meder, the most enterprising buyer of Ostades that day, had to pay to call it his. An excellent connoisseur tells us that the earliest impressions of Ostades are generally light in tone — that good impressions are also often printed in a brownish ink, and that they are without the thick line which invariably surrounds the later ones.

Wenceslaus Hollar, born at Prague in 1607, and working a long while in London, under the patronage of Charles the First's Lord Arundel, and dying here amongst us, in Gardiner Street, Westminster, in 1677, was a far more prolific etcher than either Claude, Vandyke, or Adrian Van Ostade. In fact, that is not the way to put it at all; for whilst the plates of each of these are to be counted at the most by scores, the plates of Hollar mount to the number of two thousand seven hundred. He was a craftsman of great variety and ingenuity of method. But it has, of course, to be remembered of him that in certain figure-pieces and mythological subjects at least, he was interpreter and populariser of the inventions of another, and that in most of his interesting little views he was a dainty but unmoved chronicler of pure fact. An individual note —a wholly individual note—scarcely belongs to his rendering of landscape or to his vision of the town. Yet he is a most sterling artist—not a mere monument of industry—and his quaintness, only a part of which he derives from his theme, is undoubtedly attractive. The collector who collects his work has what is a faithful record of some of the individuals and of many of the types of Hollar's time, and a fair vision of the ordinary aspect of the outward world of Hollar's day. The man's industry was, as we have seen, colossal, and even at the best he was but ill-rewarded. Fourpence per hour was, says Mr. Heywood, the price paid to him by the booksellers.

At present it may be that there is keener relish for

42

his work in Germany than here with us in England;
but one great connoisseur, as well as fine practitioner
of Etching, of a generation not yet wholly vanished,
has extolled and collected him, praising him lately,
it is true, in terms more measured than those he
had at first employed; and another connoisseur, not
born in earlier years than Sir Seymour Haden, but
earlier cut off, not living indeed to be old—I mean
the Rev. J. J. Heywood, who has been named already
—was a devoted student of Hollar's endless labours.
He prepared in great degree the Burlington Club's
Exhibition of a large fine representative collection of
Hollar's works, in 1875, and wrote the sympathetic preface to the Catalogue. On Hollar, Parthey has long
been the chief German authority; and with Parthey
Mr. Heywood was familiar. But his own loving observation of the unremitting work of the great Bohemian
engraver of the Seventeenth Century—a wanderer in
Antwerp and in Strasburg, as well as a long resident in
London—furnished him with some material of his own,
and the Burlington Club Catalogue of such portion as
was exhibited of Hollar's great volume of production,
should be, wherever it is possible, in the hands of the
Hollar collector. It will acquaint him with very many
of the most desirable pieces, and will tell him, in a
form more compact and serviceable than Parthey's,
much about the recent resting-places of the rarer
Hollar prints. There are a few of these, of course,
which cannot pass into the hands of any private person. Of the large plate of *Edinburgh*, for example, a

thing Parthey had never seen, and which was wrought
in Hollar's later time (in 1670), there exist in all the
world but two impressions. One is at Windsor, the
other at the British Museum.

When, however, the collector has got more than two
thousand plates to choose from, and to watch and wait
for, he need not, save in sheer "cussedness," and because Humanity is built that way, trouble very much
about what is for ever inaccessible. I do not think that
even a colonial millionaire will set himself the task of
collecting Hollar *en masse*. Life is not long enough. The
task would fall more properly to a German student, since
patience would be wanted, yet more than money; but,
after half a century of work, the student would pass
from us with his self-set task still uncompleted. No:
the sensible collector wants of Hollar a compact selection. Such a group as Sir Seymour Haden exhibited at
the Fine Art Society's—along with many other plates,
representing the masters of original etching—would
form a nucleus, at all events. Divided into classes in
the following way — Topography, Portraiture, Cos-
tume, Natural History, and History, that small exhibited group included the *Antwerp Cathedral*, the
Royal Exchange, the *Nave of St. George's Chapel*,
Charles the First, *Charles the Second*, one of the plates
of the *Muffs*—I trust it was the wonderful study of five
muffs alone, with the wearer's wrists and arms just
lightly indicated—and two of the rare set of *Shells*,
which are as wonderful as the muffs for texture, but
somehow a little drier. Of the plate of the *Nave of St.*

George's Chapel, Sir Seymour says that it is the most amazing piece of " biting " that he knows, as to gradation and *finesse.* Along with these plates—if he is fortunate enough to get them—or even in place of some of them, as his taste prompts him, let the collector appropriate the sets of the *Seasons* and the *Butterflies,* the little Islington set, known sometimes as *Six Views in the North of London,* and the exquisite single plate (these topographical plates that I am recommending are all small ones) known as *London from the Top of Arundel House.* Of the "simple probity" of Hollar's work, and of its rightful charm, there will then be ample evidence.

The prices of good Hollars have not of late years risen much: certainly not much in comparison with those of other prints holding positions of about the like honour. Much of his work, therefore, is quite within the reach of modest and intelligent buyers. The latest really remarkable collection sold was that of Seymour Haden, who had long possessed many more of Hollar's prints than he found room to exhibit, with other men's work, in Bond Street. His greatest rarities—perhaps even his best impressions—fetched good prices, but they were never sensational: indeed, in several instances they did not substantially exceed those realised twenty-three years earlier (in 1868), at Julian Marshall's sale. Thus, at the Julian Marshall sale, the *Long View of Greenwich* passed under the hammer at £1, 15s., and at the Haden sale it sold for £2, 5s. *London from the Top of Arundel House,* an impression of singular excellence, fetched £6 in the Marshall sale; it fetched at the Seymour Haden £9, 12s.; but in this case there is reason to suppose that Sir Seymour's impression, though certainly good, was not equal to Mr. Marshall's. *Sir Thomas Challoner* (after Holbein) fetched £31, 10s. at the Marshall sale, and I am not sure that it was not the very same impression that afterwards, at Sir Seymour's, fetched only £20. Each is described as a "First State," and each had belonged in the last century to one of the greatest collectors of his time, John Barnard, whose initials, written in a slow round hand, "J. B.," delight the collector, often, at the back of a fine print. The two impressions of *Sir Thomas Challoner* were surely really one. The portrait of *Hollar*, holding his portrait of St. Catherine, reached £6 at the Marshall sale; only £5 at the Haden. On the other hand, the *Chalice*, which is said, generally, to be from a design by Mantegna, was sold for £3, 10s. with Mr. Marshall's things; for £5, 5s. with Sir Seymour's. We need not make further comparisons; but it will be well to end these comments upon Hollar's money value by some little additional quotation from the priced catalogues of the later and larger sale of his prints. *The Rake's Lament* fetched in 1891 £22; the *Antwerp Cathedral*, in the First State, £8; that neat little set of six *Views about Islington*, £2, 10s. (which, if the impressions were all good, was unquestionably cheap); the *Royal Exchange*, in the First State, £16; *The Winter Habit of an English Gentleman*, £8, 10s.; the set of *Sea Shells*, or, rather thirty-four out of the thirty-eight numbers that the set contains, £67. Hollar, with such a mass of work to choose from, and with the interest and excellence of much of it, appeals to the collector who can dispense, at times, with vehemence and passion, and who finds in quaintness and exactness, in steady technical achievement, some compensation for the absence of a vision of exalted beauty.

CHAPTER III

THAT great old connoisseur of Rouen, Eugène Dutuit, in his two portly tomes, the *Œuvre Complet de Rembrandt* (produced in 1883), catalogues for the convenience of the collector three hundred and sixty-three pieces, though, from his long and careful Introduction, it is evident that he is not altogether uninfluenced by modern views, and is willing to discard some few out of that great array of prints. Wilson, the first important English cataloguer, working in 1836, had catalogued three hundred and sixty-nine. Charles Blanc, about a score of years later, had reduced the number to three hundred and fifty - three. Again,

in 1879, the Rev. C. H. Middleton-Wake had brought
the number down to three hundred and twenty-nine.
It is hardly likely that before the present chapter is
completed—a chapter that must be devoted mainly
to the more fascinating works of the greatest mind that
ever expressed itself in Etching—I shall have said anything of value on what is, for the student, an important
question—the question of how much of Rembrandt's
long-accepted work the master really executed. For not
in a part only of a single chapter of a volume on Fine
Prints could it be possible to deal satisfactorily with the
arguments for and against certain etchings, the authenticity of which modern Criticism disputes or doubts about.
The matter would require not paragraphs, but a volume.
Furthermore, for anything approaching a final settle-
ment, it would need such opportunities for comparison
as absolutely no one has yet been able to possess. Sir
Seymour Haden, whose views upon the subject are more
defined than most people's—if likewise it happens that
they are more revolutionary—has been pleading for a
large Exhibition and a committee of experts to settle
the matter, and, at this time of writing, the Exhibition
has not been held nor the committee formed. In regard
to its decision, I anticipate as likely to be delivered
somewhat earlier, and perhaps with more of unanimity,
the utterance of Rome upon that question of "Angli-
can Orders," which now either vexes or sympathetically
engages her.

But if the moment of connoisseurs' agreement upon
the question of the precise number of Rembrandt's true

etchings seems yet remote, the beginner in the study of the prints of Rembrandt may note with benefit two things : first, that there does exist the reasonable and long-sustained doubt in regard principally to the " Beggar " and a few of the Sacred Subjects (for certain landscapes were discarded long ago), and that thus a question has arisen into which the student may inquire cautiously, and, after much preliminary study, exercise his own mind upon ; and, second (and here comes in immediate comfort for the collector), that the doubts thrown on two or three score of prints still leave untouched the plates in which intelligent Criticism has recognised masterpieces. Again, and for his further joy, if the collector be but a beginner, or with a purse not deep, he may note that the masterpieces of Rembrandt are of the most various degrees of rarity ; that accordingly they differ inexpressibly as to the money value that attaches to them ; and that therefore, even now-a-days, though the complete or comprehensive collector of Rembrandt will have to be a rich man, a poor man may yet buy, two or three times in every year, some Rembrandt etching, noble in conception, exquisite in workmanship.

A volume like the present is not concerned primarily with the acquisitions of the millionaire, though it has, of course, to take account of them. Let us therefore, just at this stage, ask ourselves what the careful, modestly-equipped buyer does well to do, so that in his portfolios so great a master as Rembrandt shall not be altogether unrepresented, and shall not be repre-

sented unworthily? Ought the beginner to confine
himself at first to making a selection from one or two
groups only, out of the number of groups into which,
unless chronological order is to over-ride everything,
the prints of Rembrandt not unnaturally divide themselves? Or ought he to be guided in his choice by
some ascertained facts of Rembrandt's history, and by
the help of dated plates—or by accepting as fixed and
final the conjectures as to date which have proceeded
from the newer connoisseurship—seek some representation of the art of Rembrandt at different times of his
career? Or ought he, instead of either confining himself to one or two groups or classes of subject, or seek-
ing to trace at all, by the few prints of which he may
possess himself, the course of Rembrandt's progress, the
changes in his method, see rather that in his portfolios all classes of subject shall have something to
represent them, so that at least in this manner the
range of the master—which is one of the most marked
of his characteristics—shall be suggested?

The chronological plan, though it has reason on its
side and great advantages, and naturally commends
itself to the advanced student who is far already on the
road to be himself an expert, is scarcely good for the
beginner; and this not only because the proper basis
of knowledge—the date that is not a shrewd guess, but
a quite certain fact—is often wanting; but also because
the master's methods in etching, as in painting, were so
many, and in a measure at least (even the most varied
of them) were contemporaneously exercised, that the

attempt to represent periods and manners in a collection numerically insignificant becomes Quixotic or Academic. Perhaps, then, the wisest thing is to take one or two great typical groups. For my own part, I should take Portraiture and Landscape ; not of course cramping oneself with such ridiculous limitations as " Portraits of Men," " Portraits of Women "—as if the two, save for convenience of reference, should not invariably be considered together.

I have said, for one of my two groups, Landscape. I justify it by the indisputable pre-eminence which Rembrandt's etched landscapes enjoy. Even in the dignified and tasteful work of Claude there are only two or three pieces which hold their own in fascination when the memory is charged with the achievements of the Dutchman—a magical effect won out of material intractable, or at the best simple ; for that, at most, was Rembrandt's scenery. The landscape etchings of Rembrandt's compatriots, when they come to be measured by his own, assert only topographical accuracy, or faithful persevering study, or, it may be, a little manual dexterity, or their possession of a sense of prettiness which they share even with the work of the amateur. Most of the finest landscape etching of later days not only bears some signs of Rembrandt's influence, but would have been essentially other than it now is if Rembrandt's had not existed. The Dutchman's mark is laid, strong and indelible, even upon individualities so potent and distinguished as Seymour Haden and Andrew Geddes. Whistler, exquisite and peculiar as his genius is, with the figure, and with Thames-side London subjects and subjects of Venice, would, had he treated landscape proper, have either reminded us of Rembrandt, or have etched in some wrong way. He would not have etched in some wrong way—we may take that for granted; he would have reminded us of Rembrandt, with a little of himself besides.

I have shown, I think, how clearly, from the artistic point of view, the new collector is led to love and seek for Rembrandt landscapes. But there is one objection, though it is perhaps not a fatal one, to concentrating his attention upon them. Little of Rembrandt's work, except a few oddities of crazy value, like the First State of the *Hundred Guilder*, is rarer or more costly than his landscapes. Or, to be more explicit, more absolutely and literally correct, it is rather in this way: that, while for a good example of Rembrandt in any other department of his labours, it is possible of course to be obliged to give much, but likewise (Heaven be praised !) quite possible not to be obliged to give much, you will *never* without an outlay of a certain importance be possessed of any one of his landscapes in desirable condition. An outlay of £30 may conceivably endow you with a good impression of one of the two most desirable, and, as it happens, least rare, of the minor landscapes. That sum may get you, and without your having to wait a quite indefinite time for the acquisition, a *View of Amsterdam* or a *Cottage with White Palings*. It may even get you a rarer but much slighter landscape piece—that summary, though of course in its own way very learned, little performance known as *Six's Bridge;* the plate which tradition says (probably not untruly) was etched by Rembrandt while the servant of his friend, Jan Six, who had forgotten the mustard, went (somewhere beyond the pantry, however; I should even think that it was outside the house), in rapid search of that condiment.

But there, as far as landscape is concerned, if £30 or thereabouts is to be the limit of your disbursement upon a single piece, there your collecting stops. If you want a *Cottage with Dutch Hay-Barn* —very fine indeed, but not of extreme rarity—sixty, eighty, or a hundred pounds, or more, must be the ransom of it. You want a *Landscape with a Ruined Tower*—the print which, for well-considered breadth and maintained unity of effect (not so much for dainty finish) is the "last word" of landscape art, the perfect splendid phrase which nothing can appropriately follow, after which there is of necessity declension, if not collapse—it will be a mere accident if fifty guineas gets it for you. It may cost you a couple of hundred. And when? Why, only when a fine collection comes into the market: such a collection as Mr. Holford's, three or four years ago, or one at least not at all points inferior to it. And that happens not many times in the life of any one of us. Again, there is the *Goldweigher's Field,* a bird's-eye view of a plain near the Zuyder Zee; a summary, learned memorandum of the estate and

country-house, with all its appurtenances, of Uyten-
bogaert, the Receiver-General, of whom there is a
representation amongst the Rembrandt portraits. If
you can afford it, and if fortune smiles upon you by
bestowing opportunity of acquisition, you will want
not only the less costly portrait of the *Goldweigher*,
but the landscape of the *Goldweigher's Field*. There
are rarer things than that in Rembrandt's work—not
much that is more desirable. £44 was paid for an
impression, probably not quite of the first order, at the
Firmin-Didot sale, £54 at the Liphart, £72 at the
Holford. The landscapes yet more difficult to find,
command, of course, even higher prices, and this somewhat independently of their artistic interest, which
only in a very few cases—and then with very exceptional impressions—equals that of the prints I have
already named.

Of these yet rarer landscapes, as well as the other
ones, Mr. Holford's collection was certainly the finest
dispersed in recent times. His sale took place at
Christie's in July 1893 ; and at it, for the *View of
Omval*—an exceptionally splendid impression of a somewhat favourite yet not extraordinarily rare subject—
£320 was paid by M. Bouillon. The subject, though
in impressions of very different quality, had been sold
in the Sir Abraham Hume sale for £47, and in the
Duke of Buccleuch's for £44. £170 was paid for the
Three Trees, the one Rembrandt landscape which has
a touch of the sensational, which adds to its real
merit the obvious and immediate attractiveness of the

dramatic effect. Herr Meder, the dealer of Berlin, bought the First State of *The Three Cottages* for £275. The sum of £210 was the ransom of the First State of the slightly arched print *A Village with the Square Tower*. The impression, which was from the Aylesford collection, was of unparalleled brilliance, and the State is of extraordinary rarity, though M. Dutuit notes its presence at Amsterdam and at the British Museum. To M. Bouillon was knocked down for £260 a faultless impression of *The Canal*, a print which at the Galichon sale had passed under the hammer for £80, and even at the Buccleuch for £120. Messrs. Colnaghi bought for £145 a most sparkling impression of the rare First State of the broadly treated *Landscape with a Ruined Tower*, more properly called by the French cataloguers *Paysage à la Tour*, for in this First State there is no sign of "ruin." Doubtless when the title by which it is known in England was first applied to it, the amateur was unfamiliar with this rarest State, in which the dome of the tower is intact. In the Second State it has disappeared, and in the Third there are other minor changes. The reader will remember that already, two or three pages back, I have referred to this print as a masterpiece, than which none is more desirable or more representative. A perfect impression of the *Landscape with a Flock of Sheep* (from the John Barnard collection) sold for £245; the First State of the *Landscape with an Obelisk* for £185; an *Orchard with a Barn* (the early State, before the plate was cut at either end) for £170; and the First State of the

Landscape with a Boat—an impression extraordinarily full of " bur "—for £200. Altogether, the Rembrandts in the Holford sale—and I shall have to refer to some of them again before I finish the chapter—sold for £16,000. Richard Fisher's Rembrandts had fetched about £1500; Sir Abraham Hume's, £4000; Sir Seymour Haden's, £4700; the Duke of Buccleuch's, something over £10,000. The last is a figure which was never expected to be surpassed—hardly, perhaps, to be equalled. Yet it was surpassed very much.

But now it is high time I said a little about the desirableness of Rembrandt portraits and about their money value. No engraved portraiture in all the world, not even the mezzotints after Sir Joshua, present with so much power so great a range of varied character. For an artistic treatment of Humanity equally sterling and austere, you must go back to Holbein's drawings. For a variety as engaging, a vividness and flexibility as sure of their effect, only the pastels by La Tour in the Museum of St. Quentin rival these Rembrandt records of Jew and Gentile, old and young, and rich and poor in Amsterdam.

As in painting, so in etching, Rembrandt was himself one of his best models. In no less than thirty-four of his prints—according to the Catalogue of Wilson—do we find he has portrayed, at different ages, his homely, striking, penetrating face. Sometimes he is a youth ; sometimes the burden of experience is visibly laid on him ; sometimes he is engrossed with work, as in the superb *Rembrandt Drawing* ; sometimes, as in the *Rembrandt with a Sabre*, masquerading; sometimes he is depicted with great fulness of record; sometimes, as in the admirable little rarity, Wilson 364 (not catalogued amongst the Rembrandt portraits, because the plate has other heads as well), a few lines, chosen with the alacrity and certainty of genius, bring him before us, sturdy, sagacious, and with mind bent upon a problem he is sure to solve. The *Rembrandt with a Sabre*, at the Holford sale—a thing almost unique—fell to the bid of M. Deprez of £2000, and has joined now the other extraordinary possessions of Baron Edmond De Rothschild. At the Holford sale, the *Rembrandt with a Turned-up Hat and Embroidered Mantle*—an almost unique First State, drawn on by Rembrandt, but none the better on that account— fetched £420. Of the *Rembrandt Drawing* there were two impressions. One of them, which Mr. Middleton-Wake assures us is the First, and which Wilson justly describes as at all events "the finest," sold for £280 to Herr Meder. The impression was of unmatched brilliancy and vigour, the whole thing as spontaneous and im-pulsive as anything in Rembrandt's work. The second impression sold—an impression to which the honours of a true Second State are now assigned—fetched £82, and was borne away by Mr. Gutekunst of Stuttgart.

That famous Holford sale, in which, as I have said already, the *Rembrandt with the Sabre* sold for a couple of thousand, and in which the "Hundred Guilder" (*Christ Healing the Sick*) beat at least its own record, and was sold for £1750, contained among the portraits

an impression of the elaborate *Ephraim Bonus*, "with
the black ring," the only one with this singular and
somewhat petty distinction which could ever come
into the market; the remaining impressions being tied
up permanently at the British Museum and the Bibliothèque Nationale. M. Danlos took it across the
Channel, having paid £1950 for the opportunity of
doing so. The *Burgomaster Six*, an almost mezzotint-
like portrait in general effect—highly wrought, and
with an obvious delicacy—always fetches a high price.
At the Holford sale an impression called "Second
State" fell to Colnaghi's bid of £380. At the Seymour Haden, one called a "Third"—a very exquisite
impression—reached £390. It came from the collection
of Sir Abraham Hume, and Sir Seymour, in the Preface
to his sale catalogue, properly pointed out that with
the *Six*, as with the *Ephraim Bonus*, what are practically trial-proofs have been erected into "States." The
Third State of the *Old Haaring*, a portrait of a
venerable, kindly, perhaps ceremonious gentleman, who
practised the profession of an auctioneer, is scarcely
less rare than the rest. When found among the Holford treasures, it sold for £190.

For nearly the same price the benign portrait of
John Lutma, the goldsmith — an impression in the
First State, however, "before the window and the
bottle"—passed into the hands of the same buyer.
That plate—one of the most admirable in the work of
Rembrandt—affords, in its First State, an instance of the
artificial advantage of mere rarity. Because certain

collectors are accustomed to see it more or less worn, with the window and the bottle behind the seated figure, they will never give for it, even when it is not worn—if the window and the bottle happen to be there—one-third the sum that they pay willingly when those objects are absent, which Rembrandt knew were wanted to complete the composition. Now, in the case of the *Great Jewish Bride*—a portrait really of Rembrandt's wife, Saskia, with flowing hair — the background is a loss, clearly, the earlier State being invariably the finer and the more spontaneous. With the *Lutma* it is not so. There is no doubt that the additions add charm, add luminousness, to the general effect; but the fine eye is wanted, the eye of the real expert, to see to it that the impression which contains these is yet an impression in which deterioration is not visible—that it is, in fact, one of the very earliest impressions after the additions had been made.

To make an end of the record of great prices fetched by the portraits in the Holford sale, let it be said that the *Cornelius Sylvius*—the impression Wilson pronounced to be the finest—sold for £450 ; that a Second State of the rare, and on that account, as I suppose, the favourite portrait of the Advocate *Van Tolling*, fetched £530 ; whilst an exceedingly effective impression of the big portrait of *Coppenol*, the writing-master, realised no less than £1350.

But without touching any one of these great rarities, modest collectors, whose modesty yet does not go the length of making them satisfied with second-rate Art,

may still have noble portraits. Six or seven guineas—
I mean, of course, when opportunity arises—secures
you the quite exquisite and delicately modelled *croquis*
(but is it not, after all, something more than a *croquis?*)
called *Portrait of a Woman, lightly etched.* Rembrandt was very young when he did that, yet his art
was mature, his point unspeakably vivacious. It is a
portrait of his mother. So again, the *Mère de Rembrandt au voile noir*—the lady sitting, somewhat austere
this time, with set mouth, and the old full-veined
hands folded in rest—never, I think, in its happiest
impression costs more than £20—may very likely cost
you a good deal less. Ten guineas will very likely be
the ransom of that charming portrait of a boy-child in
profile, which was once thought to record the features
of Titus, Rembrandt's son, and then those of the little
Prince of Orange. It is a delightful vision of youth,
demure and chubby, and in its dainty drawing of light
and silky hair, does even Whistler's *Fanny Leyland* rival
it? Are you disposed to venture £30, £40, £50?
Then may you, in due time, add to your group a
First State of the most subtle portrait of that medita-
tive print-seller, *Clément de Jonghe.* It is treated with
singular breadth and luminousness, and of character
it is a profound revelation. By the time the Third
State is reached—and a good Third State may
be worth fifteen or twenty pounds—the thing has
changed. Indeed, it has changed already a little in
the Second. But in the Third, further work has
endowed the personage with the air of a more visible

romance; and in the two succeeding States this is preserved, though the wear of course becomes perceptible. It is well, by way of contrast, to possess yourself of this more sentimental record—the Third, if possible, in preference to the Fourth or Fifth state—besides, of course, that subtler and far finer vision of the personage which is ensured by the First State alone. The time may soon be upon us when a First State of *Clément de Jonghe* will be worth, not thirty or forty, but sixty or eighty guineas. It has always been appreciated, but it has not yet been appreciated at its true worth. Nothing in all the great etched work of Rembrandt is in craftsmanship more unobtrusively magnificent, and in its suggestion of complex character nothing is more subtle.

It was well, perhaps, to insist particularly on the desirableness, for study and possession, of these two great branches of the etched work of Rembrandt, the Landscapes and the Portraits. It would be ridiculous to attack the authenticity of any piece that I have mentioned. No one, so far as I am aware, has ever thought of doing so; so that with these, at all events, as well as with many others, the collector is safe. But my insistence on the things I have selected will not deter explorers from adventures that interest them. The unction, the vividness, and the essential dignity even of those Sacred Subjects from which he is at first repelled by the presence there so abundantly of the ungainly and the common, will in the end attract the collector. He will recognise that there was pathos in

the life Rembrandt imagined, as well as in the life that he observed. And in the Academical studies, the representations of the Nude, he will recognise that there is Style constantly, and beauty now and then. One or two of these, at least, he will like to have, if he can. Two of them seem to me better and more desirable than the rest. One is that study of a recumbent woman—*Naked Woman seen from behind*—which the French sometimes call *Négresse couchée*; but she is not "Negress" at all, but only a stripped woman beheld in deepish shadow. This is one of the least rare. Five or six pounds will often buy it. The other is the *Woman with the Arrow*. A slimmer, lighter, younger woman than is usual with Rembrandt, sits, with figure turned prettily, on the edge of a bed. The drawing is not academically perfect, but the picture is at least living flesh, graceful of pose, and seen in an admirable arrangement of shadow and of light. This *Woman with the Arrow* fetched, in the Kalle sale, £26; in the Knowles sale, £32.

The so-called "Free Subjects" are few, and the rudest of them, *Ledikant*, which has yet a touch of comedy in it (for Rembrandt was an observer always), is fortunately of extreme rarity. With not a single one of these ought the collector to be concerned. Some French artists have known how to make their choice of such subjects pardonable by treating them with grace; but the eroticism of Rembrandt—happily most occasional—is, in the very grossness of its obvious comedy, recking with offence.

In regard to the arrangement of the prints by the master who is the head and front of the Dutch school, and the consummate practitioner of Etching—I mean, the arrangement in the student's mind, and not only the arrangement in the solander box—the question of the artist's method of execution plays a not unimportant part. Are you to classify your possessions in order of date, or in accordance with subject, or with reference to style and manner of work? That third method, however, would be found in its result not very different from the arrangement by date. Broadly speaking, it would have affinity with that. For, as Sir Seymour Haden tells us in an interesting Lecture called "Rembrandt True and False," which the Macmillans issued in 1895, the Burlington Club Exhibition was itself sufficient "to disclose the interesting fact that, dividing the thirty years of Rembrandt's etching career into three parts or decades, his plates during the first of these decades were for the most part etched— "bitten in," that is, by a mordant—in the second, that after having been so bitten in, their effect was enhanced by the addition of "dry-point;" and in the third, that, discarding altogether the colder chemical process, the artist had generally depended on the more painter-like employment of "dry-point alone." And in regard to methods of work, Sir Seymour in this Lecture discredited the statement that Rembrandt was full of mysterious contrivances, and that his success as an etcher owed much to these. "All the great painter-engravers, in common with all great artists, worked

64

simply and with the simplest tools. It is only the mechanical engraver and copyist who depends for what he calls his 'quality' on a multiplicity of instrumental aids which, in fact, do the work for him—the object of the whole of them being to make that work as easy to an assistant as to the engraver himself, and its inevitable effect, to reduce that which was once an art to the level of a *métier*."

CHAPTER IV

BETWEEN the period of the work of Rembrandt and the
middle of the Eighteenth Century very little fine work
was done in Etching. The practitioners of the art,
such as they were, seemed to lose sight of its greater
principles. What they lacked in learning and in
mastery, they made up for—so they probably thought
—by elaboration and prettiness. Only here and there
did such a man as our English Geddes—our Scottish
Geddes, if the word is liked better—and he not later
than the second and third decades of our own century
—produce either portrait or landscape in the true
method, with seeming spontaneity, with means econo-
mised. It was in landscape chiefly—most particularly
in *On Peckham Rye* and *Halliford-on-Thames*—that
Geddes most successfully asserted himself, as, in his

smaller way, Rembrandt's true follower, though in his few portraits (his mother's, perhaps, most notably) the right decisiveness, simplicity, and energy of manner may not be overlooked. In some measure, it may be supposed, Geddes influenced David Wilkie, who was his friend, and Wilkie, amongst several etchings which were inferior at least to the dry-points of his fellow-workman (for his small portfolio is not, on the whole, worth much), produced one or two memorable things: a perfect little *genre* piece, called *The Receipt*—an old-world gentleman searching in a bureau, while a messenger waits respectfully at his side—being by far the best, and obviously a desirable possession.

But the middle of our century had to be reached before the true revival of the art of Etching, anywhere. Before it, Ingres, in a single plate, practised the art in the spirit of the line-engraver. Just as it approached, Delacroix and Paul Huet and Théodore Rousseau showed, in a few plates, some appreciation of the fact that etching is often serviceable chiefly as the medium for a sketch. But the middle of the century had actually to arrive before the world was in possession of the best performances of Millet, Méryon, Bracquemond, and Jules Jacquemart.

Jean François Millet executed but one-and-twenty etchings, according to the Catalogue of Monsieur Lebrun, the friend and relative of Sensier, Millet's biographer. Of M. Lebrun's Catalogue — originally issued as an Appendix to the Paris edition of Sensier's

Life of the artist—Mr. Frederick Keppel, of New York, has published a translation, with some additional facts which are of interest to the precise student. The etchings of Millet are, at the very least, masterly notes of motives for his painted pictures. But they are often much more than that. Often they are entirely satisfactory and final and elucidatory dealings with the themes they choose to tackle. They are then, quite as much as the pictures themselves, records of peasant life, as the artist observed it intimately, and at the same time vivid and expressive suggestions of atmosphere and light and shade. In effect they are large and simple. In Etching, Millet was scarcely concerned to display a skill that was very obvious, a sleight-of-hand, an acrobatic triumph over technical difficulties. Etching was to him a vehicle for the expression of exactly the same things as those to which he addressed himself in mediums more habitual. And so we have his *Glaneuses* and his *Bêcheurs*, his *Départ pour le Travail*—worth perhaps, each one of them, in good state, a very few pounds each. In America Millet has of late years been particularly appreciated. I should dare to say even that he has been overrated, owing to a skilfully-worked craze about his painted pictures, ending with the immense, ridiculous sensation of the sale of the *Angelus*. But in France—which, in the appreciation of all work of art, is certainly not less enlightened, but is cooler and more questioning—Millet is also appreciated ; nor, in England, in 1891, was there substantial difficulty in borrowing for the Burlington

Club Exhibition of the French Revival of Etching, the eleven prints, lent by Mr. Justice Day, Sir Hickman Bacon, Mr. H. S. Theobald, and Mr. Alfred Higgins, which were deemed a sufficient representation of Millet's work with the needle.

In that Exhibition the representation of the great work of Méryon was confined to twenty-five prints. It practically included all his masterpieces; but it would have been made more extensive had not the Burlington Club, soon after I published the first edition of my little book upon this master—and when Burty's Memoir was yet fresh—organised a splendid gathering of the prints we owe to Méryon's high imagination, keen sensitiveness, and unstinted labour.

I am not concerned to deal here at any length with the story of Méryon's life, or with the analysis of his poetic temperament. The question asked about him by the reader of this present book is a comparatively simple one, but I shall have to answer it with fulness—which to possess of the "sombre epics," and lovely lyrics, wrought during the time in which his spirit was most brilliant and his hand firmest?

Méryon's fame rests on the achievements of a very few years. The period comprised between 1850 and 1854 saw the production, not indeed of everything he did which may deserve to live, but of all that is sufficient to ensure life for the rest. Many of his pretty and carefully planned drawings were made earlier than 1850, and several of the more engaging of his etchings were made after 1854; but the four years between these dates were the years in which he conceived and executed his "Paris," which was something more than a collection of etched views—it was a poem and a satirical commentary on the life he recorded. Moreover, Méryon is quite pre-eminently the etcher of one great theme. Among richly endowed artists who have looked at Life broadly, it is rare and difficult to discover one whose work has evidenced such faithful concentration. It is rare enough to find that concentration even in the labour of such artists as are comparatively unimaginative, of such as are content to confine themselves to the patient record of the thing that actually is—of such an engraver, say, as Hollar. It is doubly rare to find an imaginative artist of wide outlook and of deep experience so much the recorder of one set of facts, one series of visions. He will generally have been anxious to give form to very different impressions that came to him at various times and under changing circumstances. Now it may have been Landscape that interested him, and now Portraiture, and now again ideal composition or traditional romance. And in each he may have fairly succeeded. But Méryon, though stress of circumstance obliged him to do work beyond the limits of his choice, did such work, generally speaking, with only too little of promptings from within, to lighten the dulness of the task. There are, of course, exceptions—one or two in his Landscape, if there are none in his Portraiture. But the beginning and the end of his art, as far as the world can be asked to be seriously concerned with it, lay in the imaginative

70

record, now faithfully simple, now transfigured and
nobly visionary, of the city which requited him but ill
for his devotion to its most poetic and its most prosaic
features. It is the etchings of Paris, then, that the
collector will naturally first seek.

Nearly all the etchings of Paris are included in what
is sometimes known as "the published set." Not that
the twelve major and the eleven minor pieces comprised
in that were ever really published by fashionable print-
sellers to an inquiring and eager public. But they
were at least so arranged and put together that this
might have happened had Méryon's star been a lucky
one. In Méryon's mind they constituted a "work," to
which the few other Parisian subjects afterwards came
as a not unsuitable addition. Like the plates of
"Liber Studiorum," they were to be looked at "together." Together, the plates of "Liber" represented,
as we shall see better in another chapter, the range of
Turner's art. Together, the etchings "sur Paris"—
"on" and not "of" Paris, let it be noted—represented
Méryon's vision of the town, and of its deeper life.

In beginning a collection of Méryon's, I imagine it
to be important not only to begin with one of the
"Paris," but with a very significant example of it—a
typical, important etching. The twelve views—the
twelve "pictures," I should prefer to call them—
Méryon himself numbered, when, rather late in life, he
issued the last impressions of them. These numbered
impressions, being, as I say, the very last States, are
not the impressions to cherish; but these are the

subjects of them (and the subjects, in finer impressions, will all be wanted)—the *Stryge*, the *Petit Pont*, the *Arche du Pont Nôtre-Dame*, the *Galerie de Nôtre-Dame*, the *Tour de l'Horloge*, the *Tourelle*, *Rue de la Tixéranderie*, the *St. Etienne-du-Mont*, the *Pompe Nôtre-Dame*, the *Pont Neuf*, the *Pont-au-Change*, the *Morgue*, and, lastly, the *Abside de Nôtre-Dame*. Before these, between them, and again at the end of them, are certain minor designs, not to be confused with that "Minor Work," chiefly copies and dull Portraiture, described but briefly in my little book on Méryon, which is devoted more particularly to the work of genius with which it is worth while to be concerned. Those minor designs which are associated with the "Paris" are an essential part of it, doing humble, but, as I am certain Méryon thought, most necessary service. In a sense they may be called head-pieces and tail-pieces to the greater subjects of which the list lies above. Sometimes they are ornament, but always significant, symbolic ornament; sometimes they are direct, written commentary. Either way, they bear upon the whole, but yet are less important than those twelve pieces already named. So it was, at all events, in Méryon's mind; but of one or two of them it is true also that they have a beauty and perfection within their limited scheme, lacking to one or two of the more important, to which they serve humbly as page or out-rider. The one lyric note of the *Rue des Mauvais Garçons*, for instance, is in its own way as complete a thing as is the magnificent epic of *Abside* or *Morgue*—

it is greater far than the *Pompe Nôtre-Dame*, or, it may be, than the *Petit Pont*. The late Mr. P. G. Hamerton—an admirable specialist in Etching, but a writer making no claim to the narrower speciality of minute acquaintance with Méryon—has praised the *Pompe Nôtre-Dame*. He has praised it for merits which exist, and it is only relatively that the praise is, as it seems to me, undeserved. The plate is really a wonderful victory over technical difficulties; but, in the ugly lines of it, its realism is realism of too bold an order. The *Petit Pont* is a fine piece of architectural draughtsmanship, and an impressive conception to boot; but, like Rembrandt's wonderfully wrought *Mill*, it is one-sided—it wants symmetry of composition.

The *Abside* is accounted the masterpiece of Méryon, in right of its solemn and austere beauty. A rich and delicate impression of this print is, then, the crown of any Méryon collection. It must be obtained in a State before the dainty detail of the apse of the cathedral, and the yet daintier and more magically delicate workmanship of its roof, in soft and radiant light, have suffered deterioration through wear. It must be richly printed. The First State is practically not to be found. I suppose that there are scarcely in existence seven or eight impressions of it. It is at the British Museum, and in the collections of Mr. B. B. Macgeorge, Mr. Avery, Mr. Mansfield, Mr. R. C. Fisher, and Mr. Pyke Thompson. For the last that changed hands, fully 125 guineas was paid. Méryon had received for it—and gratefully, in his depression

73

and poverty—one shilling and threepence. I have seen his receipt. But money now will not acquire it. A Second State is therefore the one to aim at; and, just because there were so very few impressions taken of the First, that I ought, in my Catalogue, to have described them as proofs—more especially as there was no change whatever in the work, but only in the lettering—it stands to reason that the earliest and best impressions of the Second (I mean these only) are, in their exquisite quality, all that good judges can desire. These are on thin and wiry paper—old Dutch or French—often a little cockled. The green, or greenish, paper Méryon was fond of, he never used for the *Abside*. The poorer impressions of the Second State are on thick modern paper. After the Second State, which, when carefully chosen, is apt to be so beautiful—and is worth, then, forty or fifty guineas—there comes a Third, a Fourth, a Fifth: none, fortunately, common; and deteriorations, all of them; downward steps in the passage from noble Art to the miserable issue of a thing which can rejoice the soul no longer, nor evidence the triumph of the hand.

Not much more need be said in detail here as to the larger prints of the great "Paris," but there is still a little. In the shape and size of the plate, and by its breadth of distant view, the *Pont-au-Change* is the companion to the *Abside*. There are some impressions on the greenish paper, and some on the thin Dutch that yields the best of the *Absides*. The im-

pression of the First State in the De Salicis Sale sold
for £33. The *Pont-au-Change* is one of those prints
which have submitted to the most serious alterations.
A wild flight of giant birds against the rolling sky is
the first innovation—it occurs in the Second State—
and though it removes from the picture all its early
calm and half its sanity, it has, as many think, a charm
of its own, a weird suggestiveness. A good impression,
in this State, is worth, it may be, £6 or £7. The next
change—when the flight of birds gives place to a flight
of small balloons (unlike the large balloon which, in the
First State, sails nobly through the sky, before ever the
dark birds get there)—the next change, I say, is a
more pronounced mistake. The *Tour de l'Horloge*—
of which a First State fetched in the Wasset Sale £10,
and in the De Salicis £22—has also submitted to
change, but scarcely in a State in which it need
occupy the careful collector. In certain late impressions, Méryon, convinced, in the restlessness of mental
ill-health, that one side of the tall Palais de Justice was
left in his picture monotonous and dull, shot great
shafts of light across it, and these became the things
that caught the eye. He had forgotten, then, the
earlier wisdom and more consummate art by which,
when first he wrought the plate, he had placed the
quiet space of shadowed building as a foil to the
many-paned window by the side of it. The change
is an instructive and pathetic commentary on the
ease with which artistic conceptions slip away, they
themselves forgotten, and the excellence that they

had beautifully achieved ignored even by the mind that gave them birth.

The *St. Etienne-du-Mont* is one of those etchings which possess the abiding charm of perfect things. In it a subject entirely beautiful and dignified is treated with force and with refinement of spirit, and with faultless exactitude of hand. It shows—nothing can better show—the characteristic of Méryon, the union of the courage of realism and the sentiment of poetry; in other words, its realism, like the realism of the finest Fiction, has to be poetic. You have the builder's scaffolding, the workmen's figures, for modern life and labour; the Gothic stones of the Collège de Montaigu, the shadow of the narrow street, the closely-draped women hurrying on their way, for old-world sentiment and the mystery of the town. But I suppose a chapter might be written upon its excellent beauty. I mention it here, partly because it too submits to change, though change less important than that in the *Pont-au-Change*, and less destructive than that in the *Tour de l'Horloge*. Not to speak of sundry inscriptions, sundry "posters," which Méryon, in mere restlessness, was minded to alter, he could never quite satisfy himself about the attitude of one of the workmen on the scaffolding. Three States represent as many changes in this figure, and all these—as a matter, at all events, of minor interest—it is pleasant to collect. Here, in the *St. Etienne*, as so often in the etchings of Méryon, the First State (£16 in the De Salicis Sale) is the one of which the impressions are the most

76

numerous, though even in this piece of writing, which
does not take the place of a catalogue, I have had
occasion to note one instance out of some in which it
is not so. But generally it is so. And so the Méryon
collector has to be even more careful than the collector
of " Liber" about the impression which he buys. He
must have an early State, but it is not enough to have
an early State. He must most diligently teach himself
to perceive what is really a fine example of it. He
must not fall into the commonest vice of the unintelligent purchaser—be captivated by the mere word,
forego his own judgment, and buy First States with
dull determination.

Presently the collector of the " Paris " will legitimately want the smaller pieces, some of which I have
called " tail-pieces": all are commentaries and con-
necting-links. Some are beautiful, complete, and significant, as has already been said, but generally the
significance is more remarkable than the beauty. They
bind together, almost as an appropriate text itself
might bind together, what might otherwise be detached
pictures. They complete the thought of Méryon in
regard to his " Paris," and make its expression clear.
Thus, the etched cover for the Paris Set bears the title,
" Eaux Fortes sur Paris," on a representation of a slab
of fossiliferous limestone, suggesting the material which
made it possible to build the city on the spot where
it stands. Then, there is a set of etched verses wholly
without other ornament than may be found in their
prettily-fantastic form, verses that bewail the life of

Paris. Again, lines to accompany the *Pont-au-Change* and its great balloon. These things recall William Blake—the method by which the " Songs of Innocence " first found their limited public. Again, the *Tombeau de Molière*—Méryon thinks there must be place in his Paris for the one representative French writer of imaginative Literature, the cynic, analyst, comedian. And to name one other little print, but not to exhaust the list, there is a graceful embodiment of wayward fancy to accompany the *Pompe Nôtre - Dame*. It is called the *Petite Pompe*—represents the Pompe in small ; gives us verses regretting half playfully, half affectionately, the removal of so familiar a landmark, and surrounds all with a flowing border of rare elegance and simple invention.

But a few other brilliant and poetical records of Paris lie, it has been said already, outside the published Set, claim a place almost with the greater illustrations I have spoken of earlier, and must surely be sought. The *Tourelle, dite " de Marat "* is one of these, and it is Méryon's record of the place where Charlotte Corday did the deed by which we remember her. Except for the interest of observing a change, due, I may suppose, to the dulled imagination of a fairly shrewd tradesman —a change by which all symbolism and significance passed out of this wonderful little print—it is useless to have this little etching in any State after the First published one. For, after the First published one, the picture and the poem became merely a view : there is nothing to connect the place with Marat's tragedy,

and Méryon has been permitted to represent, not
the Tourelle, dite "de Marat," but "No. 22, Street
of the School of Medicine." And the First State is
already rare. There were very few impressions of it.
It was too imaginative for the public. But here is
an instance in which Trial Proofs, generally to be
avoided, may fairly be sought for, along with the First
State. Distributed among different collectors is a
little succession of Trial Proofs with different dates of
May and June written by Méryon in pencil on the
margin. The first and second belong to Mr. Macgeorge; the third was Seymour Haden's; the fourth
belongs to Mr. James Knowles; the eighth—which is the
last—belongs to me (I got it, if I recollect, for £8, 10s.
and a commission, at the Wasset Sale). Even at the
beginning of this little sequence of proofs the work
is not ineffective; and at the end it is complete.

Also outside the published Set of "Paris" are two
little etchings which are particularly noteworthy, and
which, by reason of the extreme, even astounding, delicacy of some of their work, it is, I think, well to secure
in the early state of Trial Proof—when one can get the
chance. These are the *Pont-au-Change vers* 1784—
which no one can possibly confuse with the larger *Pont-
au-Change*—and *Le Pont Neuf et la Samaritaine*. Unlike most of Méryon's Parisian work, both are, not
indeed transcripts from, but idealisations of, drawings
by another. The first dry draughtsman, in the present
case, was one Nicolle. As far as the practical presenta-
tion of all the subject is concerned, the Trial Proofs of

these prints, which have been sold under the hammer
for about £10 each, are all that can be wanted, and
they possess, moreover, an exquisite refinement of
light, of which the published, and especially the later
published, examples give no hint. All impressions of
these two little plates are worthy of respect, for these
plates were never worked down to the wrecks and
skeletons of some of the others; but, nevertheless, it is
only in the earliest impressions that we can fully see
the lovely lines and light and shade of the background
in the *Pont-au-Change vers* 1784—it must be had
"before the great dark rope"—and the sunlit house-
fronts (Van der Heyden-like, almost) of the *Pont Neuf
et la Samaritaine*.

Of the Bourges etchings, which are good, though
none are of the first importance—and they are but few
in all—the best is the *Rue des Toiles*. It is a varied
picture, admirably finished. The rest are engaging
sketches.

Amongst the remaining etchings by which Méryon
commends himself to those who study and reflect upon
his work, it is enough, perhaps, here, to speak of three.
Océanie: Pêche aux Palmes is almost the only quite
satisfactory record of that acquaintance that he made
with the antipodes. The Second State—with the title—
is not scarce at all, and can never be costly. You may
pay, perhaps, one or two pounds for it, and for the first,
say, four or five. The *Entrée du Couvent des Capucins
Français à Athènes*—a print devoted in reality to the
Choragic Monument of Lysicrates—is the single and the

very noble plate which a visit to Athens, when he was a sailor, inspired Méryon to produce. This rare plate was done for a book that is itself now rare—Count Léon de Laborde's "Athènes au XVme, XVIme, et XVIIme Siècles." Even in the Second State the *Entrée du Couvent* has fetched about £12, in more sales than one. *Rochoux's Address Card*, albeit not particularly rare, is curious and worth study. It was executed for the only dealer who substantially encouraged Méryon; and Méryon contrived to press into his little plate much of what he had already found and shown to be suggestive in the features of Paris. Symbolical figures of the Seine and Marne recline at the top of the design. Then there are introduced bits from the *Arms of Paris*, from the *Bain Froid Chevrier* (the statue of Henri Quatre), from *Le Pont Neuf*, and from *La Petite Pompe*. No one, of course, can ask us to consider *Rochoux's Address Card* very beautiful or grandly imaginative; but it is ingenious, and, like *La Petite Pompe*, though in more limited measure, it is good as a piece of decorative design.

The impressions of Méryon's etchings are printed on papers of very different sorts. A greenish paper Méryon himself liked, and it is one of the favourites of collectors. Its unearthly hue adds to the weirdness of several of the pictures, often most suitably; but it is not always good. Méryon knew this, and many of his plates—amongst them, as I have said already, that unsurpassable masterpiece, the *Abside*— were never printed on it. I have a *Rue des Mauvais*

Garçons—the thing was Baudelaire's favourite—upon
very blueish gray. A thin old Dutch paper, wiry and
strong, white originally and softened by age, gives
some of the finest impressions. Other good examples
are on Japanese, and there are fine ones on thinnest
India paper that is of excellent quality. Modern
Whatman and modern French paper have been used
for many plates; and a few impressions, which, I think,
were rarely, if ever, printed by any one but Méryon
himself, are found on a paper of dull walnut colour.
If I seem to dwell on this too much, let it be remembered that very different effects are produced by the
different papers and the different inks. The luxurious
collector, possessing more than one impression, likes
to look first at his "Black *Morgue*," and then at his
"Brown." The two make different pictures.

About the Méryon collections, it may be said that
M. Niel, an early friend, possessed the first important
group that was sold under the hammer. Then followed
M. Burty's, M. Hirsch's, and afterwards M. Sensier's.
These fetched but modest prices—prices insignificant
sometimes—for Méryon's vogue was not yet. Later,
the possessions of M. Wasset—an aged bachelor, eager
and trembling, whom I shall always remember as the
"Cousin Pons" of certain *bric-à-brac*-crowded upper
chambers in the Rue Jacob—were sold for more substantial sums. Since then, the collection of that most
sympathetic amateur, the Rev. J. J. Heywood—one of
the first men in London to buy the master's prints—
has passed into the hands of Mr. B. B. Macgeorge of

Glasgow, whose cabinet, enriched from other sources, is now certainly the greatest. The Méryons that belonged to Sir Seymour Haden went, some years since, to America, where whoever possesses them must recognise collectors that are his equals, in Mr. Samuel Avery and Mr. Howard Mansfield. If too many carefully gathered groups of Méryon's etchings have left our shores, others remain — though very few. The British Museum Print-Room is rich in the works of the master: many of the best impressions of his prints, there, having belonged long ago to Philippe Burty, who early recognised something at least of their merit, and made, in the *Gazette des Beaux Arts* of that day, the first rough catalogue of them.

It is time we turned for a few minutes to Felix Bracquemond—a dozen years Méryon's junior, for he was born in 1833. Among the sub-headings to this present chapter there occurs the phrase, "Bracquemond's few noble things." Why "few"?—it may be asked—when, in the Catalogue of the Burlington Club Exhibition of the French Revival of Etching, it is mentioned that the number of his plates extends to about seven hundred, and that the list would have been longer had not Bracquemond, in his later years, accepted an official post which left him little time for this department of work? Well, there are two or three reasons why, with all respect to an indefatigable artist, I still say "few." To begin with, no inconsiderable proportion of Felix Bracquemond's etched plates are works of reproduction—translations (like

Rajon's, Waltner's, Unger's, some indeed of Jacquemart's) of the conceptions of another. These may be admirable in their own way—the *Erasmus*, after the Holbein, in the Louvre, is more than admirable: it is masterly—a monument of austere, firmly-directed labour, recording worthily Holbein's own searching draughtsmanship and profound and final vision of human character. But we have agreed, throughout the greater part of this book, and more especially in those sections of it which are devoted to the art whose greatest charm is often in its spontaneity, to consider original work and work inspired or dictated by others as on a different level. Then again, in such of Bracquemond's prints as are original, there is perhaps even less than is usual, in a fine artist's work, of uniformity of excellence. No very great number of all the plates M. Beraldi industriously chronicles need the collector busy himself with trying to acquire. The largish etchings of great birds, alive or dead, are amongst the most characteristic. With singular freedom and richness—an enjoyment of their plumage and their life, and a great pictorial sense to boot—has Bracquemond rendered them. If I could possess but a single Bracquemond—I have none, as a matter of fact—I would have such an impression of *Le Haut d'un Battant de Porte*, with the birds hanging there, as Mr. Alfred Morrison lent to the Burlington Club. The plate was wrought in 1865. But *Margot la Critique* and *Vanneaux et Sarcelles*—prints of, I think, about the same period —likewise represent the artist well; and there is a

plate done only about nine years ago, at the instance
of the Messrs. Dowdeswell, which is certainly a triumph
at once of *technique* and of character. This is *Le
Vieux Coq.*

Daubigny, Maxime Lalanne, Meissonier, Corot, are
all amongst French artists who have etched, and have
etched more or less ably. The two last-mentioned—
doubtless the most important artists in their own customary mediums—wrought the fewest plates. Corot's
are highly characteristic sketches. Daubigny worked
more systematically at etching, and you feel in all his
works a sympathetic, picturesque vision of Nature; but
his prints never reach exquisiteness. Lalanne, who
was extremely prolific with the needle, had an unfailing
elegance as well as facility. And, as a little practical
treatise that he wrote upon the subject shows, he was
devoted to the craft. He was best in his smaller
plates: never, I think, having beaten his dainty plate
of the Swiss *Fribourg*, which was given in "Etching
and Etchers." Seen in large numbers, his prints reveal,
if not exactly mannerism, at least the quickly reached
limits of his personality. In the portfolios of the
collector, a few prints—which will never cost many
shillings—are enough to represent him. But I have
no wish whatever to underrate Lalanne, in saying this.
Lalanne was not a great artist; but he was an agreeable, well-bred observer, and a graceful draughtsman.

A genius, wholly individual of course, or he would
not be a genius at all—and yet in a sense the founder of
a school or centre of a group of workmen—now occupies

us. We pass to Jules Jacquemart, who, born in 1837, died prematurely in 1880; a child of his century, worn out by eager restlessness of spirit, by the temperament, by the nervous system, that made possible to him the exquisiteness of his work. The son of a collector, a great authority on porcelain, Albert Jacquemart, Jules Jacquemart's natural sensitiveness to beauty, which he had inherited, was, from the first, highly cultivated. From the first, he breathed the air of Art. Short as his life was, he was happy in the fact that adequate fortune gave him the liberty, in health, of choosing his work, and, in sickness, of taking his rest. With extremely rare exceptions, he did the things that he was fitted to do, and did them perfectly; and, being ill when he had done them, he betook himself to the exquisite South, where colour is, and light—the things we long for most, when we are most tired in cities—and so there came to him, towards the end, a new surprise of pleasure in so beautiful a world. He was happy in being surrounded, all his life long, by passionate affection in the circle of his home. Nor was he perhaps unhappy altogether, dying in middle age. For what might the Future have held for him?—a genius who was ripe so soon. The years of deterioration and of decay, in which first an artist does but dully reproduce the spontaneous work of his youth, and then is sterile altogether—the years in which he is no longer the fashion at all, but only the landmark or the finger-post of a fashion that is past—the years when a name once familiar and honoured is uttered at rare intervals and in tones of apology, as the name of one whose performance has never quite equalled the promise he had aforetime given—these years never came to Jules Jacquemart. He was spared these years.

But few people care, or are likely to care very much, for the things which chiefly interested him, and which he reproduced in his art; and even the care for these things, where it does exist, unfortunately by no means implies the power to appreciate the art by which they are retained and diffused. "Still-life"—the portrayal of objects natural or artificial, for the objects' sake, and not as background or accessory—has never been rated very highly or very widely loved. The public generally has been indifferent to these things, and often the public has been right in its indifference, for often these things are done in a poor spirit, a spirit of servile imitation or servile flattery, with which Art has little to do. But there are exceptions, and there is a better way of looking at these things. Chardin was one of these exceptions—in Painting, he was the greatest of these. Jacquemart, in his art of Etching, was an exception not less brilliant and peculiar. He and Chardin have done something to endow the beholders of their work with a new sense—with the capacity for new experiences of enjoyment—they have portrayed, not so much matter, as the very soul of matter; they have put it in its finest light, and it has got new dignity. Chardin did this with his peaches and his pears, his big coarse bottles, his copper sauce-pans, and his silk-lined caskets. Jacquemart did it with the

87

finer work of artistic men in household matter and
ornament: with his blue and white porcelain, with his
polished steel of chased armour and sword-blade, with
his Renaissance mirrors, and his precious vessels of
crystal, jasper, and jade. But when he was most fully
himself, his work most characteristic and individual,
he shut himself off from popularity. Even untrained
observers could accept this agile engraver as the interpreter of other men's pictures—of Meissonier's inventions, or Van der Meer's, Greuze's, or Fragonard's—but
they could not accept him as the interpreter, at first
hand, of treasures peculiarly his own. They were not
alive to the wonders that have been done in the world
by the hands of artistic men. How could they be
alive to the wonders of this their reproduction—their
translation, rather, and a very free and personal one—
into the subtle lines, the graduated darks, the soft or
sparkling lights of the artist in Etching?

A short period of practice in draughtsmanship, and
only a small experience of the particular business of
etching, made Jacquemart a master. As time proceeded, he of course developed; found new methods,
ways not previously known to him. But little of what
is obviously tentative and immature is to be noticed
even in his earliest work. He springs into his art an
artist fully armed—like Rembrandt with the wonderful portrait of his mother "lightly etched." In 1860,
when he is but twenty-three, he is at work upon the
illustrations to his father's "Histoire de la Porcelaine,"
and though, in that publication, the absolute realisation

of wonderful matter—or, more particularly, the breadth in treating it—is not so noteworthy as in the later "Gemmes et Joyaux de la Couronne," there is most evident already the hand of the delicate artist and the eye that can appreciate and render almost unconsidered beauties.

The "Histoire de la Porcelaine" contains twenty-six plates, of which a large proportion are devoted to the Oriental china possessed in mass by the elder Jacquemart, when as yet there was no rage for it. Many of Albert Jacquemart's pieces figure in the book : they were pieces the son had lived with and knew familiarly. Their charm, their delicacy, he perfectly represented—nay, exalted—passing without sense of difficulty from the bizarre ornamentation of the East to the ordered forms and satisfying symmetry which the high taste of the Renaissance gave to its products. Thus, in the "Histoire de la Porcelaine"—amongst the quaintly naturalistic decorations from China and amongst the ornaments of Sèvres, with their boudoir graces and airs of pretty luxury fit for the Marquise of Louis Quinze and the sleek young Abbé, her pet and her counsellor, we find, rendered with an appreciation as just, a *Brocca Italienne*, the Brocca of the Medicis of the Sixteenth Century, slight and tall, where the lightest of Renaissance forms the thin and reed-like *arabesque*—no mass or splash of colour—is patterned over the smoothish surface with measured exactitude and rhythmic completeness. How much is here suggested, and how little done ! The actual touches are almost as

few as those which Jacquemart employed afterwards in
rendering some fairy effects of rock-crystal—the material
which he has interpreted, it may be, best of all. On
such work may be bestowed, amongst much other
praise, that particular praise which seems the highest
to fashionable French Criticism—delighted especially
with feats of adroitness: occupied with the evidence of
the artist's dexterity—"*Il n'y a rien, et il y a tout.*"

The "Histoire de la Porcelaine"—of which the
separate plates were begun, as I have said before, in
1860, and which was published by Techener in 1862—
was followed in 1864 by the "Gemmes et Joyaux de
Couronne." The Chalcographie of the Louvre—which
concerns itself with the issue of State-commissioned
prints—undertook the first publication of the "Gemmes
et Joyaux." In this series there are sixty subjects, or,
at least, sixty plates, for sometimes Jacquemart, seated
by his Louvre window (which is reflected over and over
again at every angle, in the lustre of the objects he was
drawing), would etch in one plate the portraits of two
treasures, glad to give "value" to the virtues of the
one by juxtaposition with the virtues of the other;
opposing, say, the transparent brilliance of the globe
of rock-crystal to the texture and hues, sombre and
velvety, of the vase of ancient sardonyx, as one puts
a cluster of diamonds round a fine cat's-eye, or a black
pearl, glowing soberly.

Of all these plates M. Louise Gonse has given an
accurate account, in enough detail for the purposes of
most people, in the "Gazette des Beaux Arts" for

1876. The Catalogue of Jacquemart's etchings—which are about four hundred in all—there contained, was a work of industry and of very genuine interest on M. Gonse's part, but its necessary extent, due to the artist's own prodigious diligence in work, cannot for ever sufficiently excuse an occasional incompleteness of description making absolute identification sometimes a difficult matter. The critical appreciation was warm and intelligent, and the student of Jules Jacquemart must always be indebted to Gonse. But for the quite adequate description of work like Jacquemart's—the very subject of it, quite as much as the treatment—there was needed not only the French tongue (the tongue, *par excellence*, of Criticism), but a Gautier to use it.

Everything that Jacquemart could do in the rendering of beautiful matter, and of its artistic and appropriate ornament, is represented in one or other of the varied subjects of the " Gemmes et Joyaux," save only his work with delicate china. And the large plates of this series evince his strength, and hardly ever betray his weakness. He was not, perhaps, a thoroughly trained Academical draughtsman; a large and detailed treatment of the nude figure—any further treatment of it than that required for the beautiful suggestion of it as it occurs on Renaissance mirror-frames or in Renaissance porcelains—might have found him deficient. He had an admirable feeling for the unbroken flow of its line, for its suppleness, for the figure's harmonious movement. He was not the master of its most intricate anatomy; but, on the scale on which he had to treat it, his suggestion was faultless. By the brief shorthand of his art in this matter, we are brought back to the old formula of praise. Here, indeed, if anywhere, "*Il n'y a rien, et il y a tout.*"

As nothing in Jacquemart's etchings is more adroit than his treatment of the figure, so nothing is more delightful and, as it were, unexpected. He feels the intricate unity of its curve and flow—how it gives value by its happy undulations of line to the fixed, invariable ornament of Renaissance decoration—an ornament as orderly as well-observed verse, with its settled form, its repetition, its refrain. I will name one or two notable instances. One occurs in the etching of a Renaissance mirror (the print a most desirable little possession)—*Miroir Français du Seizième Siècle*, elaborately carved, but its chief grace after all is in its fine proportions—not so much the perfection of the ornament as the perfect disposition of it. The absolutely satisfactory filling of a given space with the enrichments of design, the occupation of the space without the crowding of it—for that is what is meant by the perfect disposition of ornament—has always been the problem for the decorative artist. Recent fashion has insisted, sufficiently, that it has been best solved by the Japanese; and indeed the Japanese have solved it, often with great economy of means, suggesting, rather than achieving, the occupation of the space they have worked upon. But the best Renaissance Design has solved the problem as well, in fashions less arbitrary, with rhythm

92

more pronounced and yet more subtle, with a precision more exquisite, with a complete comprehension of the value of quietude, of the importance of rest. If it requires—as Francis Turner Palgrave said, admirably —"an Athenian tribunal" to understand Ingres and Flaxman, it needs at all events high education in the beauty of line to understand the art of Renaissance Ornament. Such art Jacquemart understood absolutely, and, against its purposed rigidity, its free play of the nude figure is indicated with touches dainty, faultless, and few. Thus it is, I say, in the *Miroir Français du Seizième Siècle*. And to the attraction of the figure has been added almost the attraction of landscape and of landscape atmosphere in the plate No. 27 of the "Gemmes et Joyaux" which represents scenes from Ovid as a craftsman of the Renaissance has portrayed them on the delicate liquid surface of *cristal de roche*. And not confining our examination wholly to "Gemmes et Joyaux," of which, obviously, the mirror just spoken of cannot form a part—we observe there, or elsewhere in Jacquemart's prints, how his treatment of the figure takes constant note of the material in which the first artist, his original, worked. Is it raised porcelain, for instance, or soft ivory, or smooth, cool bronze with its less close and subtle following of the figure's curves, its certain measure of angularity in limb and trunk, its many facets, with a somewhat marked transition from one to the other (instead of the unbroken harmony of the real figure), its occasional flatnesses? If it is this, this is what Jacquemart gives us in his etchings—not the figure only, but the figure as it comes to us through the medium of bronze. See, for example, the *Vénus Marine*, outstretched, with slender legs—a bronze, long the possession of M. Thiers, I believe. One really cannot insist too much on Jacquemart's mastery over his material—*cloisonné*, with its rich, low tones, its patterning outlined by its metal ribs; the coarseness of rough wood, as in the *Salière de Troyes*; the sharp, steel weapons and the infinite delicacy of their lines, as in *Epées, Langues de Bœuf, Poignards*; the signet's flatness and delicate smoothness—"c'est le sinet du Roy Saint Louis"—and the red porphyry, flaked, as it were, and speckled, of an ancient vase; and the clear, soft, unctuous green of jade.

And as the material is marvellously varied, so are its combinations curious and wayward. I saw, one autumn, at Lyons, their sombre little church of Ainay, a Christian edifice built of no Gothic stones, but placed, already ages ago, on the site of a Roman Temple—the Temple used, its dark columns cut across, its black stones re-arranged, and so the Church completed—Antiquity pressed into the service of the Middle Age. Jacquemart, dealing with the precious objects that he had to portray, came often on such strange meetings: an antique vase of sardonyx, say, infinitely precious, mounted and altered in the Twelfth Century, for the service of the Mass, and so, beset with gold and jewels, offered by its possessor to the Abbey of Saint Denis.

It was not a literal translation, it must be said again, that Jacquemart made of these things. These things sat to him for their portraits; he posed them; he composed them aright. Placed by him in their best lights, they revealed their finest qualities. Some people bore hardly on him for the colour, warmth, and life he introduced into his etchings. They wanted a colder, a more impersonal, a more precise record. Jacquemart never sacrificed precision when precision was of the essence of the business, but he did not—scarcely even in his earlier plates of the " Porcelaine "—care for it for its own sake. And the thing that his first critics blamed him for doing—the composition of a subject, the rejection of this, the choice of that, the bestowal of fire and life upon matter dead to the common eye— is a thing which artists in all arts have always done, and for this most simple reason, that the doing of it is Art.

As an interpreter of other men's pictures, it fell to the lot of Jacquemart to engrave the most various masters. But with so very personal an artist as he, the interpretation of so many men, and in so many years, from 1860 or thereabouts, onwards, could not possibly be of equal value. As far as Dutch Painting is concerned, he is strongest when he interprets, as in one now celebrated etching, Van der Meer of Delft. *Der Soldat und das lachende Mädchen* was, when Jacquemart etched it, one of the most noteworthy pieces in the cabinet of M. Léopold Double. It was brought afterwards to London by the charming friend of many artists and collectors—the late Samuel Joseph—in the hands of whose family it of course rests. The big and

95

blustering trooper common in Dutch art, sits here, engaging the attention of that thin-faced and *cveillée* maiden peculiar to Van der Meer. Behind the two, who are contentedly occupied in gazing and talk, is the bare, sunlit wall, spread only with its map or chart, and, by the side of the couple, throwing its brilliant but modulated light upon the woman's face and on the background, is the intricately patterned window, the airy lattice. Rarely was a master's subject, or his method, better interpreted than in this print. The print possesses, along with all its subtlety, a quality of boldness demanded specially by Van der Meer, and lacking to prints which in their imperturbable delibera-tion and cold skill render well enough some others of the Dutch masters—I mean the Eighteenth Century line engravings of J. G. Wille after Metsu and the rest.

Frans Hals, once or twice, is as characteristically rendered. But with these exceptions it is Jacquemart's own fellow-countrymen whom he translates the best. The suppleness of his talent—the happy speed of it, not its patient elaboration—is shown by his renderings of Greuze: the *Rêve d'Amour*, a single head, and *L'Orage*, a memorandum of a young and frightened mother, kneeling by her child, exposed to the storm. Greuze, with his cajoling art—which, if one likes, one must like without respecting it—is entirely there. So, too, Fragonard — the ardent and voluptuous soul of him—in *Le Premier Baiser*.

Jacquemart, it may be interesting to add, etched some compositions of flowers. Gonse has praised them. To me, elegant as they are, fragile of substance, dainty of arrangement, they seem enormously inferior to that last century flower-piece of Jan Van Huysum's — or rather to that reproduction of it which we are fortunate enough to know through the mezzotint of Earlom. And Jacquemart painted in water-colour—made very clever sketches: his strange dexterity of handling, at the service of fact; not at the service of imagination. In leaving him, it is well to recollect that he recorded Nature, and did not exalt or interpret it. He interpreted Art. He was alive, more than any one has been alive before, to all the wonders that have been wrought in the world by the hands of artistic men.

I have not said a word about the prices of the Jacquemart etchings. It is still customary to buy a complete series—one particular work. The " Porcelaine " set costs a very few pounds : the " Gemmes et Joyaux," something more—and Techener's re-issue, it is worth observing, is better printed than the first edition. Separate impressions of the plates, in proof or rare states, sell at sums varying from five shillings or half-a-sovereign—when scarcely anybody happens to be at Sotheby's who understands them — up, I suppose, to two or three pounds. I do not think the acquisition of these admirable pieces is ever likely to be held responsible for a collector's ruin.

In the Introductory chapter, a word of reference to two other Frenchmen — Legros and Paul Helleu —points to the importance which, in contemporary

original Etching, I assign to these artists. As Legros
has lived nearly all his working life in England, he
is treated, in subsequent pages, with English fellow-
workers. Even Paul Helleu I treated with English-
men, in my book called "Etching in England,"
because he also has done some part—though a small
part — of his work here, and has been one of the
mainstays of our Society of Painter - Etchers. But
in the present volume—for the purposes of the Collector—Helleu must be placed with his compatriots.
The character of his genius too — his alertness and
sensitiveness to the charm of grace rather than of
formal beauty, the charm of quick and pretty movement rather than of abiding line — is French, essentially. He is of the succession of Watteau. His
dry-points, of many of the best of which there are
but a handful of impressions (purchasable, when occasion offers, at three or four guineas apiece), are
artist's snap-shots, which arrest the figure suddenly
in some delightful turn, the face in some delightful
expression. Am I to mention but two examples of
Paul Helleu's work—that I may guide the novice a
little to what to see and seek for in these elegant,
veracious records — I will name then *Femme à la
Tasse*, with its happy and audacious ingenuity in
point of view, and that incomparable *Étude de Jeune
Fille*, the girl with the hair massed high above her
forehead, thick above her ears, a very cascade at
her shoulders, her lips a little parted, and her lifted
arms close against her chin.

FRENCH REVIVAL OF ETCHING

A Belgian draughtsman—established in Paris, and now approaching old age—has seen of late his reputation extending, not only amongst collectors of the cleverly odious; and he has shown imagination, draughtsmanship, a nimble hand, a certain mastery of process. But in a volume from which I must exclude so much of even wholly creditable Art—a volume in which the subject of Woodcuts, which of old was wont to interest, is deliberately ignored—I adopt no attitude of apology for refusing serious analysis to the too often morbid talent of Félicien Rops. A portfolio containing the delightful inventions of Helleu, and the great things of Méryon, could have no place for the record of Rops' disordered dream. Were I to be occupied with any living Belgian, it would be with one whose work M. Hymans, the Keeper of the Prints at Brussels, showed me at the Bibliothèque Royale, this autumn—M. de Witte.

CHAPTER V

In England, the Revival of Etching, so far as one can fix its origin at all, seems due, in chief, to the great practical work of two etchers of individual vision and exceptional power — Whistler and Seymour Haden. Much writing on the subject—and some of it, I hope, not bad—has also scarcely been without its effect. It has at least roused and sustained some interest in Etching, amongst the public that reads. It cannot, fairly, ever have been expected to produce great artists.

Whistler and Haden are, it is now allowed, amongst the Classics already. Each has a place that will not be disturbed. Each is an honoured veteran. The work of Seymour Haden has been closed long ago. It is years since he gave his etching-needle to Mr. Keppel of New York; saying, with significant gesture, " I shall etch no more." From the other delightful veteran no such

formal declaration has—so far as I understand—as yet
proceeded. Mr. Whistler may even now surprise us by
a return from Lithography. His lithographs, which
will be considered more or less in the final chapter of
this book, are indeed admirable and engaging. But
it is by his etchings that Mr. Whistler's fame will
live. And though he began to etch two score of years
ago, one would be sorry even now to feel it was quite
certain that the last of his etchings had been done.

We will speak of Seymour Haden first. He is the
older of the two, and his practical work is admittedly
over. His etching, though conceived always on fine
lines, has somehow always been much more intelligible
to the large public than Whistler's. For years, in
England and America, he has enjoyed something as
near to popular success as sterling work can ever get ;
and in days when I was able to pick up for six shillings,
in Sotheby's auction-rooms, the dry-point of Whistler's
Fanny Leyland—which would now be considered ridiculously cheap at just as many guineas—Seymour Haden's
River in Ireland was selling (when it appeared and
could be bought at all) at quite substantial prices.
His published series of Etchings, with the text by Monsieur Burty, and then the eulogies of Mr. Hamerton,
had done something, and justifiably, towards what is
called "success"—the success of recognition, I mean,
as distinguished from the success of achievement, which
was certainly his besides. And then—in the nick of time
—there had come the *Agamemnon*, almost the largest
fine etching one can call to mind ; for, in Etching,

" important size " often means vulgarity. The *Agamemnon* had an immense sale. It was seen about so much, in the rooms of people who aspired to Taste, that it became what foolish men call " vulgarised." As if the multiplication of excellent work—its presence in many places, instead of only a few—was positively a nuisance and a disadvantage ! Anyhow, Seymour Haden had already entered into fame.

In 1880, the late Sir William Drake—an intimate friend who had collected Haden and admired him— issued, through the Macmillans, a descriptive Catalogue of Haden's etched work. The Catalogue takes note of a hundred and eighty-five pieces. Scarcely anything, I think, is omitted. Of the substantial work none bears an earlier date than 1858; but fifteen years before that—when he was a very young man, journeying—Haden had scratched on half-a-dozen little coppers sparse notes of places of interest he had seen in Italy ; and very long ago now (when Sir Seymour was living in Hertford Street) he showed me, I remember, the almost unique impressions from these practically unknown little plates. They were impressions upon which a touch or so with the brush had—if I remember rightly—a little fortified the dreamy and delicate sketch which the copper had received. There is neither need nor disposition to insist too much on the existence of these plates, or rather upon the fact that once they were wrought. They scarcely claim to have merit. But the fact that they were wrought shows one thing a collector may like to know—it shows that Seymour

102

Haden's interest in Etching began before the days of that French Revival in which was executed undoubtedly the bulk of his work.

These little prints, then, as far as they went, were in quite the right spirit. They were jottings, impressions —had nothing of labour in them. But in the interval that divides them from the important and substantive work of 1858, 1859, 1860, and later years, the artist must have studied closely, though he was in full practice, most of that time, as a surgeon. In the interval, he had lived, so to put it, with Rembrandt; he had become familiar with Claude. And though they influenced, they did not overpower him. By 1864, there were fifty or sixty prints for M. Burty to chronicle and eulogise, in the *Gazette des Beaux Arts*. The greatly praised *Shere Mill Pond* had been done in 1860. *Mytton Hall*—which, unlike Mr. Hamerton, I prefer to the *Shere*—had been wrought one year earlier. It shows a shady avenue of yew-trees leading to an old manor-house which receives the full light of the sun; and in that print, early as it may seem, there was already the breadth of treatment which as years proceeded became more and more a characteristic of Seymour Haden's work. In 1863 came, amongst many other good things, *Battersea Reach*, which in the First State bore on it this inscription of interest: "Old Chelsea, Seymour Haden, 1863, out of Whistler's window." To the same year belongs the charming plate, *Whistler's House, Old Chelsea*. The tide is out, the mud is exposed; on the left is Lindsay Row; and

beyond, and to the right, Chelsea Old Church and
Battersea Bridge: the picturesque wooden pile-bridge
of that privileged day. It was not till 1870 that
there came the *Agamemnon*—the *Breaking-up of the
Agamemnon*, to give it its full title—a view, in reality,
of the Thames at Greenwich, seen under sunset light,
the hull of the old ship partially swung round by the
tide. This very favourite print exists in a couple
of States. The Second, though less rare, is scarcely
perceptibly less fine than the First. In it a smoking
chimney, a brig under sail, and two small sailing-boats
—all of them objects in extreme distance—have been
replaced by indications of the sheds of a dockyard. In
the Heywood Sale, a rich impression of the *Agamemnon*
—the State not specified, but in all probability a First
—sold for £7, 10s. In the Sir William Drake Sale,
twelve years afterwards—in 1892—a First State fetched
£7, 7s.; a Second, £6, 15s.

For convenience' sake, I will name a few more
excellent and characteristic works — prints which
have Seymour Haden's most distinguishing qualities
of frankness, directness, and an obvious vigour. His
etchings are deliberately arrested at the stage of the
sketch; and it is a sketch conceived nobly and executed
with impulse. The tendency of the work, as Time
went on, was, as has been said, towards greater breadth;
but unless we are to compare only such a print as
Out of Study-Window, say (done in 1859), with only
the most admirable Rembrandt-like, Geddes-like dry-
print, *Windmill Hill* (done in 1877), there is no greatly

marked contrast; there is no surprise; there is but a steady and not unnatural development. I put this down, in part at least, to the fact that when Seymour Haden first took up Etching seriously (in 1858, remember) he was already middle-aged. He had lived for years in the most frequent intercourse with dignified Art; his view of Nature, and of the way of rendering her—or of letting her inspire you—was large, and likely to be large. Yet as Time went on there came no doubt an increasing love of the sense of spaciousness and of potent effect. The work was apt to be more dramatic and more moving. The hand asked the opportunity for the fuller exercise of its freedom.

Sawley Abbey, etched in 1873, is an instance of this, and not alone for its merits is it interesting to mention it, but because, like a certain number of its fellows amongst that later work, it is etched upon zinc—a risky substance, which succeeds admirably, when it succeeds, and when it fails, fails very much. *Windmill Hill*—two subjects of that name—*Nine Barrow Down*, *Wareham Bridge*, and the *Little Boathouse*, and again that *Grim Spain* which illustrates my " Four Masters of Etching " are the prints which I should most choose to possess amongst those of Haden's later period; whilst—going back to the period of 1864 and 1865—*Sunset on the Thames* is at the same time a favourite and strong, and *Fenton Hook* remarkable for its draughtsmanship of tree-trunk and stump. Yet earlier—for they belong to 1860 and 1859—there are the *Mytton Hall*, which I have spoken of already, and the *Combe Bottom*. *Combe Bottom* is unsurpassed for sweetness and spontaneity. And *Mytton Hall* has its full share of that priceless element of Style which is never altogether absent from Seymour Haden's work. Again—and most acceptable of all to some of us— *The Water Meadow* (which has been circulated very largely) is, in a perfect impression, to be studied and enjoyed as a vivacious, happy, sympathetic transcript of a sudden rain-storm in the Hampshire lowlands, where poplars flourish and grass grows rank. The collector who can put these things into his folios— and a little diligence in finding them out, and three or four guineas for each print, will often enable him to do so—will have given himself the opportunity of confirmation in the belief that among modern etchers of Landscape, amongst modern exponents in the art of Black and White of an artistic sympathy with pure and ordinary Nature, Seymour Haden stands easily first. And to say that, is not to say that he succeeds equally, or has equally tried to succeed, with portraiture or figure-studies. It is not to compare him —to his advantage or disadvantage—with any other artist in the matter of the etcher's peculiar skill and technical mastery.

The best collection of Seymour Haden's work that has ever been sold in detail was the collection of Sir William Drake. In it the First State of *A River in Ireland*—of which only twelve impressions had been taken—fetched £49 (Dunthorne); and the First State of *Shere Mill Pond*, £35; a unique impression of

Battersea Railway Bridge fetched £18, 10s. (Deprez);
Erith Marshes, First State, £4, 4s.; *Combe Bottom*, First State, £3; *Sunset on the Thames*, First
State, £2, 12s.; and *Sawley Abbey*, First State,
£2, 4s.

With the master-etchers of the world—Méryon's
equal in some respects, and, in some respects, Rembrandt's—there stands James Whistler. Connoisseurs
in France and England, in America, Holland, Bavaria,
concede this, now. It was fiercely contested of old
time, and there is not much cause for wonder in
that, for the work of Mr. Whistler is, and has been
from the first almost, so desperately original that the
world could hardly be expected to be ready to receive it.
And Mr. Whistler never by anything approaching to
cheap issue facilitated familiarity with his work. In
1868 Mr. Hamerton wrote of him: "I have been told
that, if application is made to Mr. Whistler for a set of
his etchings"—the set, it may be said in parenthesis,
was a very small one then—"he may perhaps, if he
chooses to answer the letter, do the applicant the
favour to let him have a copy for about the price of
a good horse; but beyond such exceptional instances
as this, Mr. Whistler's etchings are not in the market."
They have been in the market since, however—everybody knows—and if in 1868 a "set" (the Thames Set
or the French Set was meant, presumably) was valued
by Mr. Whistler at the price of a horse, of late years
a single print, such as the *Zaandam* for instance, has
been valued by Mr. Whistler at the price of a Humber

cycle. Even in the days—some sixteen years ago, or
so—when the work of the delightful master was least
appreciated, there was an enormous difference in the
price of a print obtained through what are known
as the "regular channels" and its price if obtained
in open competition, under the hammer at Sotheby's.
Those great days!—or days of great opportunities
—when, as I have said before, I became possessed
for six shillings of *Fanny Leyland*, and, for hardly
more than six shillings, of the yet rarer dry-point,
Battersea Dawn.

About a dozen years ago, I, with the enthusiasm
of a convert, began a Catalogue of Whistler's prints,
intending it for my own use. I finished it for
my brother-collectors, and for poor Mr. Thibaudeau,
who refreshed me with money—and a little for Mr.
Whistler, too, if he was minded to receive my offering.
The only previously existing Catalogue—that of Mr.
Ralph Thomas—had been published twelve years earlier,
and had meantime become of little service. There were
several reasons for that, but, to justify my own attempt
—which, as in the case of Méryon, has been justified
indeed by my brother-collectors' reception of it—it
will suffice if I mention one. Mr. Thomas, working in
1874, catalogued about eighty etchings. I, finishing
my work in 1886, catalogued two hundred and four-
teen. Of the additional number only a few are prints
which had been already wrought when Mr. Thomas
wrote, and which had escaped his notice. By far the
greater portion have been etched in more recent years.

And many of them are unknown to the amateur—by sense of sight at least—even to this day.

Whistler's etchings are so scattered, and so many of them are, and must ever be, so very rare, that I could not have done what I did if several diligent collectors, well placed for the purpose, had not helped me. Mr. Thibaudeau himself—the erudite dealer—amassed much information, and placed it at my service. Mr. Samuel Avery, when Mr. Keppel took me to see him in East 38th Street, in the autumn of 1885, put at my disposal everything he knew; and his collection was even then the worthy rival of what Mr. Howard Mansfield's is now—the rival, almost, of Seymour Haden's own collection of Whistler's, which went to America a few years ago: drawn thither by the instrumentality of a great cheque from Mr. Kennedy. Mr. Mortimer Menpes—much associated with Whistler at that time, and who, I suppose, retains the fine collection of Whistler's he then possessed—took much trouble with me in the identification of the rare things he owned, and I had to express my thanks to Mr. Barrett of Brighton, to the Reverend Stopford Brooke, Mr. Henry S. Theobald, and some of the best-known London dealers — to Mr. Brown of the Fine Art Society, and Mr. Walter Dowdeswell, an enthusiast for Whistler, who furnished me with delightful notes I never published, on the precise condition of the impressions in my own set of the "Twenty-Six Etchings." Again, I saw—what any one may see—such of the Whistler prints as are possessed by the British Museum Print-Room. And, lastly, I had access, more than once, to Mr. Whistler's own collection; but that unfortunately was very incomplete. It consisted chiefly of the later etchings.

It is now about forty years since Whistler began to etch; but his work in Etching has never been continuous or regular, and though he has done a certain number of things, some fine, some insignificant, since the appearance of my Catalogue, of late his work in Etching appears to have almost ceased. Looking back along his life, one may say, periods there have been when he was busy with needle and copper—periods, too, during which he laid them altogether aside. The first chronicled, the first completed plate, was done, it was believed, in 1857—when he was a young man in Paris. But he told me there existed, somewhere or other, in the too safe keeping of public authorities in America, a plate on which, before he left the public service of the States, he neglected to fully engrave that map or view for the Coast Survey which the authorities expected of him, but did not neglect to engrave upon the plate, in truant mood, certain sketches for his own pleasure. The plate was confiscated. Young Mr. Whistler was informed that an unwarrantable thing had been done. He perfectly agreed—he told the high official—with that observation. In removing a plate from the hands of its author before he had completed his pleasure upon it, its author had been treated unwarrantably. Just as my Catalogue—a "Study and a Catalogue," I call it—was going to press, there arrived from New York—sent thence to London by the courtesy of Mr. Kennedy, its owner—an impression from the copper I have just spoken of. It is a curiosity, and not a work of Art—a geographer's view of the coast.

It will be noticed from my little anecdote that, at a very early period of his life, Mr. Whistler was in the right, absolutely, and other people in the wrong—and in the right he has remained ever since, and has believed it, in spite of some intelligent and much unintelligent criticism. He has been (let the collector be very sure of this) a law unto himself—has worked in his own way, at his own hours, on none but his own themes: the result of it, I dare to think deliberately, the preservation of a freshness which, with artists less true to their art and their own mission, is apt to suffer and to pass away. And with it the charm passes. Now Whistler's newest work—his work of this morning, be it etching or lithograph—possesses the interest of freshness, of vivacity, of a new and beautiful impression of the world, conveyed in individual ways, just as much as did his early work of nearly forty years ago. When the comparatively few people whose artistic sensibilities allow them to really understand the delicacy of Mr. Whistler's method, shall but have known it long enough, they will not be found, as some among the not quite unappreciative are found to-day, protesting that there is a want of continuity between the earlier efforts and the later, and that the vision of pretty and curious detail, and the firmness and daintiness of hand in recording it, which confessedly distinguished the etchings of France

111

and of the Thames below Bridge, are missing to the
later plates or the plates of the middle period—to the
dry-points of what I may term the Leyland period (when
he drew all three Miss Leylands, their father and
their mother too, and *Speke Hall*, where they lived),
and to the more recent Venetian etchings. *Peccavi!*
I have myself, in my time, thought that this continuity
was wanting. I have told Mr. Whistler with exceeding
levity of speech, that when, in the Realms of the Blest,
he desired, on meeting Velasquez and Rembrandt, not
to disappoint them, he must be provided, for his justification, with his Thames etchings in their finest states.
It would be a potent introduction. But I am not
sure that the Venetian portfolios—the "Venice" and
the "Twenty-Six Etchings," which are most of them
Venetian in theme—would not serve Mr. Whistler in
good stead. For—spite of some insignificant things
put out not long after the appearance of my Catalogue,
along indeed, or almost along with some fine ones of
Brussels and Touraine—there is a continuity which the
thorough student of Mr. Whistler's work will recognise.
There is often in the Venetian things—as in the *Door-
way* of the "Venice," and in *The Garden* and *The
Balcony* of the "Twenty-Six Etchings"—an advance
in the impression produced, a greater variety and flexibility of method, a more delightful and dexterous
effacing of the means used to bring about the effect.

The Venetian etchings—some people thought at first
they were not satisfactory because they did not record
that Venice which the University-Extension-educated

tourist, with his guide-book and his volumes of Ruskin, goes out from England to see. But I doubt if Mr. Whistler troubled himself about the guides or read the sacred books of Mr. Ruskin with becoming attention. Mr. Ruskin had seen Venice nobly, with great imagination; Mr. Fergusson and a score of admirable architects had seen it learnedly; but Mr. Whistler would see it for himself—that is to say, he would see in his own way the Present, and would see it quite as certainly as the Past. The architecture of Venice had impressed folk so deeply that it was not easy in a moment to realise that here was a great draughtsman — a man too of poetic vision — whose work it had not been allowed to dominate. The Past and its record were not Whistler's affair in Venice. For him, the lines of the steam-boat, the lines of the fishing-tackle, the shadow under the squalid archway, the wayward vine of the garden, had been as fascinating, as engaging, as worthy of chronicle, as the domes of St. Mark's.

Yet we had not properly understood Mr. Whistler's work in England, if we supposed it could be otherwise. From associations of Literature and History this artist from the first had cut himself adrift. His subject was what he saw, or what he decided to see, and not anything that he had heard about it. He had dispensed from the beginning with those aids to the provocation of interest which appeal most strongly to the world— to the person of sentiment, to the literary lady, to the man in the street. We were to be interested—if we were interested at all—in the happy accidents of line

113   H

and light he had perceived, in his dexterous record, in his knowing adaptation.

I must be allowed to say, however—and it is useful to the collector that I should say it plainly—that there was some justification (much more than Mr. Whistler, I suppose, would allow) for those of us who did not bow the knee too readily before the Venetian prints. In the States in which they were first exhibited, there was, with all their merits, something ragged and disjointed about several of them. Mr. Whistler worked more upon them later, adding never of course merely finicky detail, but refinement, suavity. Of these particular plates, the collector should remember, it is not the earlier impressions that are the ones to be desired. It is, rather, the later impressions, when the plate was, first, perfected—then even, if need arose through any wear in *tirage*, suitably refreshed.

To return for a moment to Whistlerian characteristics. Though the value of many of his etchings, as Mr. Whistler might himself tell us, consists in the exquisiteness of their execution and of their arrangement of line, it would be unfair not to acknowledge that amongst the many things it has been given to Mr. Whistler to perceive, it has been given him to perceive beautiful character and exquisite line in Humanity —that, certainly, just as much as quaintness and charm in the wharves and warehouses of the Port, in the shabby elegance of the side canals of Venice, in the engaging homeliness of little Chelsea shop-fronts. The almost unknown etching of his mother—one of the most

114

refined performances of his career, as exquisite, in its
own way, as the famous painting which is displayed at
the Luxembourg—proves his possession of the quality
which permitted Rembrandt to draw with the reticence
of a convincing pathos his most impressive portraits of
the aged—the *Lutma*, the *Clément de Jonghe*, the *Mère
de Rembrandt, au voile noir*.

Again, the *Fanny Leyland*, and *The Muff*, and many
another print that I could name, attest Mr Whistler's
solution of a problem which presents itself engagingly,
attractively, to the ingenious, and uselessly to the in-
competent—the problem of seeing beauty in modern
dress, and grace in the modern figure. Whistler, no
more than Degas, Sargent, or J. J. Shannon, sighs for
the artificial dignity of the fashions of other times.
Even at moments when modern Fashion is not in truth
at its prettiest, he is able to descry a piquancy in the
contemporary hat, and to find a grace in the flutter of
flounce and frill. What else after all should we expect
from an artist the sweep of whose brush would give
distinction to the Chelsea Workhouse, or to the St.
George's Union Infirmary in the Fulham Road, and for
whom, under the veil of night or dusk, the chimney
of the Swan Brewery would wear an aspect not less
beautiful than King's College Chapel? It has been
given to the master of Etching to see everyday things
with a poetic eye.

"Take care of the extremities," said old Couture, to a
painter who addressed himself to the figure: "take care
of the extremities, for all the life is there." But that,

it may truly be answered, is what Mr. Whistler has often neglected to do. It may be rejoined, however, that where he has neglected to do it, somehow " all the life " has not gone out of his work. And the hand of the man sitting in the boat, in one of the most desirable of the early Thames etchings, *Black Lion Wharf*, and (to name no other instance) the hands in the painting of Sarasate of a dozen years ago, are reminders of how completely it is within Mr. Whistler's power to indicate the life, the temperament, by " the extremities," when it suits his work that he shall do so. And the avoidance, so often commented upon, of this detail here, and of that detail there, itself reminds us of something important—nay, perhaps of the central fact which determines the direction of so much of this great etcher's labour. It reminds us that whether Mr. Whistler's work is record of Nature or not, it has at all costs to be conclusive evidence of Art. And for the one as well as for the other, he has had need to know, not only what to do — a difficult thing enough, sometimes—but a more difficult thing yet: what to avoid doing. In other words, selection plays in his work a part unusually important, and he has occupied himself increasingly, not with the question of how to imitate and transcribe, but with the question how best to imply and to suggest. In nearly all his periods he is the master of an advanced art, which gives a curious and a various and a continual pleasure.

And now a word or two on what is matter of business to the collector—the business of the acquisition

116

of Whistler's etchings. Unlike the thousand prints which, in these later days of "the Revival," are the inadequate result of the laborious industry of popular people—and which have served their purpose when, framed and mounted, they have covered for a while the wall-paper in every builder's terrace in Bayswater—works of the individuality, the flexibility, the genius in fine of Whistler, appeal to the collector of the highest class and of the finest taste, and, it may be even, to him alone. They lie already in the portfolio by the side of Rembrandts and Méryons. It is not easy to get them; or, rather, there are some which it is only difficult, and some which it is impossible, to possess. Certain of the coppers are known to have been destroyed; others, which one cannot always particularise, are in all probability destroyed. Then again there are dry-points, never very robust; some of them so delicate, so evanescent, that the plate, should it exist, would prove to be worth nothing. It has yielded, perhaps, half-a-dozen impressions, and they have gone far towards exhausting it. Many plates, again, exist, no doubt, in the late State, or in the undesirable condition, and some are yet intact, and others, like the two Venetian series—the "Venice" and the "Twenty-Six"—economically managed from the beginning, have yielded a substantial yet never an extensive array of such proofs as satisfy the eye that is educated.

Publication—if one can quite call it so—of Mr. Whistler's etchings first began in 1859, when the artist had worked seriously for only two or three years.

Thirteen etchings, generally called "the French Set," were printed then by Delâtre in Paris, in very limited numbers, on the thin Japan or China or on the good old slightly-ribbed paper that the collector loves. The "Thames Set"—sixteen in number, and consisting of the majority of the River pieces executed up to that time—were the next to be offered. But they appeared, publicly, only in 1871, when, as Mr. Ellis was good enough to tell me, "Ellis & Green" bought the plates and had a hundred sets printed. Their printing was rather dry, so that it is chiefly by the rare impressions which either Mr. Whistler himself, or Delâtre it may be, had printed, years before, that these plates are to be judged. At all events it is these impressions which represent them most perfectly, though I would by no means speak with disrespect of the impressions printed by Mr. Goulding when the Fine Art Society bought the plates of Mr. Ellis, nor of the subsequent ones printed quite of late years, when Mr. Keppel, in his turn, bought the coppers of the Fine Art Society.

Of the two other recognised sets—the "Venice" of the Fine Art Society and the "Twenty-Six Etchings" of the Dowdeswells—it must be said first that neither has been subjected to the vicissitudes that attended the earlier plates. The dozen prints in the "Venice" were first issued by the Fine Art Society in the year 1880; but, as I have said earlier, very few of the fine and really finished impressions—of the hundred permitted from each plate—date from as early as that year. The "Twenty-Six Etchings," issued by the Messrs.

Dowdeswell, were brought out in 1886; Mr. Whistler himself printing, with consummate skill, every mortal copy, and making the most interesting little changes, repairs, improvements, at the press-side. Of most of the subjects there were but fifty impressions.

These things are wholly admirable, and mostly—it is evident—are rare; but the extremest rarity is reserved for a few of those many plates which do not belong to any set at all, and were never formally issued. Thus *Paris, Isle de la Cité*—etched from the Galérie d'Apollon in the Louvre—is of unsurpassable rarity; and it is singularly interesting as having, though with a date as early as 1859, very distinct characteristics of a style of which the wider manifestation came much later. The First State of the *Rag Gatherers* is of great, though not of quite such extraordinary rarity. The *Kitchen*, in the First State, is not exceptionally rare. It should be had, if possible, in the Second, for, many years after its first execution, Mr. Whistler took it up again, and then, and then only, was it that he perfected it. In subtlety of illumination, in that Second State, it is as fine as any painting of De Hooch's. *Westminster Bridge* is very rare and very desirable in the First State; in the Second—by which time it has gone into the regular "Thames Set" or "Sixteen Etchings"—it has lost all its delicacy and harmony: it is hard and dry. The figure-pieces of the Leyland period — dry-points, nearly always — are very rare. They include not only a little succession of portraits—the lovely print of *Fanny Leyland* I have referred

119

to already—but likewise a succession of studies of paid or of familiar models, of which the *Model Resting* is one of the most beautiful. There is *Tillie:* a model, too : likewise of great rarity and charm. Of the larger etchings, three of the finest are the *Putney Bridge,* the *Battersea Bridge,* and the *Large "Pool."* Beyond this scale, Etching can hardly safely go. Even this scale would be a danger to some, though Mr. Whistler has managed it. But then, that art of his — like Rembrandt's own — can "blow on brass" as well as "breathe through silver." He "breathes through silver" in the dainty rarities of a later time, the little Chelsea shop subjects—*Old Clothes Shop, Fruit Shop.* Are there half-a-dozen impressions of them anywhere in the world ? And then, the poetic charm of *Price's Candle Works*—the easy majesty of *London Bridge !*

As to the prices of Whistlers in the open market ? Well, they increase, unquestionably. Some of the very greatest rarities, it may be remembered, have never appeared in the auction-room. There are half-a-dozen, I suppose, for any one of which, did it appear, forty or fifty guineas would cheerfully be paid. The average price, now, of a satisfactory Whistler — to speak to the collector very roughly, and always with the difficulty of striking an average at all—the average dealer's price might now be eight guineas. But we will look at the Catalogues ; premising, as has been pre-mised already, that there are some rarer things than any that are there chronicled. The time when Mr. Heywood sold his Whistlers was the fortunate time to buy. A First State of the *Rag Gatherers* was sold then for less than two pounds; a First of the *Westminster Bridge* (then called " The Houses of Parliament"), for about five pounds; and many quite desirable things went for a pound a piece, and some for a few shillings. In 1892, when there came the sale of Mr. Hutchinson's collection, and of Sir William Drake's, opinion was more formed; yet nothing like the prices that would be reached to-day were attained then. In Mr. Hutchinson's collection, the First State of the *Marchande de Moutarde* — rare, but not especially rare — went for £4, 10s.; the First State of the *Kitchen* for £8, 15s.; the *Lime Burners* for £6, 10s.; a trial proof of the *Arthur* for £10, 15s.; a trial proof of the *Whistler* for £15, 10s. Again, the *Weary* fetched £12; the First State of *Speke Hall*, £9, 12s.; the *Fanny Leyland*, £15, 10s.; *From Pickled Herring Stairs*, £6, 6s.; the *Palaces*, £8, 15s; the *San Biagio*, £7, 10s; the *Garden*, £5, 10s.; the *Wool Carders*, £8; the *Little Drawbridge, Amsterdam*, £9, 15s.; the *Zaandam*, £10. At the Drake Sale—a smaller one, as far as Whistlers were concerned—ten guineas was given for the *Kitchen*; £19 for the *Forge*. It must be added that this *Forge*, which is in the second published set (the "Thames series" or "Sixteen Etchings," call them which you will) is in the quality of its different impressions more unequal than almost any print I know. It varies from an ineffective ghost to a thing of beauty. At £19, let us hope it was a thing of beauty; but very much oftener it is an ineffective ghost—desperately over-rated.

121

CHAPTER VI

Etchers since our great Classics—William Strang—His individuality, and obligations to Legros — That excellent Master—Legros's nobility and dignity—His observation and imagination—Holroyd—The daintiness of Short—C. J. Watson—Goff, flexible and comprehensive —The qualities of Cameron — Oliver Hall's Landscape — The question of prices — Contemporary Prints generally dear.

THOUGH no very definite commercial values may yet have been established, in the auction-rooms, for their work, many living English etchers of a generation later than that of Whistler and of Seymour Haden have been for some time now appealing to the collector; and their prints—sold chiefly perhaps at the " Painter-Etcher's," at Mr. Dunthorne's, and at Mr. R. Gutekunst's—are worthy to be carefully considered. The best of them, at least, will rank some day as only second to the classics of their art. Indeed, if the term " the Revival of Etching " has any meaning, it is to the best men of the later generation that it must most apply; for " revival " signifies surely some tolerably wide diffusion of interest, and is a word that could scarcely be used if all we were concerned with were the efforts of two or three isolated men of genius — in France, Méryon, Bracquemond, Jacquemart; in England, Haden and Whistler.

No, the collector who addresses himself to the gathering of modern etchings, must go — or may go, fairly — beyond the limits of the work of the men I have this instant named. But in going beyond them, very wary must be his steps. He who is already a serious student of the older masters—he who by happy instinct, or by that poor but necessary substitute for it, a steady application to the consideration of great models—knows something of the secrets of Style, and so will not fall a ready prey to the attractions of the meretricious and the cheap. But the beginner is in need of my warning; and among the work of the younger generation, the etching that is already popular and celebrated— more particularly the etching that is obviously elaborate and laboured—is as a rule the work he must eschew. The thing of course to aim at, is to acquire gradually such "eye" and knowledge as will enable him to pounce with safety here and there upon unknown work; but at first it is well perhaps that in his travels beyond the territory of the admittedly great, he shall not wander too far. I will give him the names of a few artists, whom the connoisseur begins to appreciate,—men of whose methods it will be interesting, and need not be extravagant, to possess a few examples.

Of any such men, here with us in England—save indeed Legros, whose claims to highest place I hold to

be yet more incontestable—William Strang is the one
who has been known the longest, though the number
of his years may still permit him, ere he pass from us,
to double the already formidable volume of his work.
Strang has etched in the right methods, and no one
knows much better than he does, the *technique* of the
craft; and, then, moreover, though he paints from
time to time a little, it is Etching—and all of it
original Etching—that is the occupation of his life.
And within less than twenty years Mr. Strang has
wrought—well, say between two hundred and fifty and
three hundred plates. It is no good giving the precise
number, for before this book has lain for a month upon
the reader's shelf the number will have ceased to be
precise. Almost as many kinds of subjects as were
treated by Rembrandt, have been treated—and no one
of them on one or two occasions only—by Mr. William
Strang. He has dealt with religious story—caring
always, like Rembrandt, and like Von Uhde to-day, for
dramatic intensity in the representation of it, rather
than for local colour—he has dealt too with Landscape,
with Portraiture, with grim and sordid aspects of contemporary life.

The presence of imagination, the absence, almost
complete, of formal beauty, are the very "notes" of
Mr. Strang's work — that absence is so remarkable
where it would have been least expected, that we are,
it may be, a little too apt to forget that in certain
of his masculine portraiture it does not make itself
felt at all. He has made etchings of handsome men,

and they have remained handsome. He has even made etchings of men not handsome, and handsome they have become. But he knows not the pretty woman. And his landscape is endowed but scantily with the beauty it cannot entirely miss. Another curious thing about Mr. Strang's landscape is, that more even than that of Legros, his first great master, it seems derived from but a little personal observation and an immense study of the elder art. Indeed, I am not quite sure whether, save in the accessories of his figures—such as the potato-basket of one of his woebegone, limping, elderly wayfarers—Mr. Strang has ever drawn and observed anything which had not already fallen within the observation of the great original engravers of the remoter Past. In his dramatic pieces he shows a sense of simple pathos, as well as of the uncanny and the weird. In Portraiture Mr. Strang can be effectively austere and suitably restrained. Occasional failures, or comparative failures, such as the portraits of Mr. Thomas Hardy and of the late Sir William Drake, do perhaps but bring into stronger relief the successes of the *Mr. Sichel* and of *Ian Strang*, and many others besides. I must refrain from naming them. When Mr. Strang has done so much, and nearly all of it on a high technical level, it is natural to feel that though out of them all the general collector of etchings might reasonably be satisfied with the possession of a dozen—or, peradventure, six—he would like at least to choose them for himself. Indeed, there is no "best" to guide him to—no "worst" to guard him against.

125

Legros has been named as Strang's first master. He belongs to an older generation, and if I name him here, between his best-known pupil and some of the younger men, it is not to minimise his importance, but in part as a convenient thing, and in part because, with his long years of English practice, one hesitates to allow even French birth and a French first education to cause one to place Legros outside the English School that he has influenced. Born at Dijon nearly sixty years ago, Legros has been amongst us since 1863. But it is not English life—or indeed any life—that has made him what he is. He might have done his work—most of it at least but the portraiture—while scarcely wandering beyond the bounds of a Hammersmith garden. He has been fed on the Renaissance, and fed on Rembrandt; but yet the originality of his mind pierces through the form it has pleased him to impose on its expression. He gives to masculine character nobility and dignity; or rather, he is impressed immensely by the presence of these things in his subjects. His etching of Mr. G. F. Watts is perhaps—taking into account both theme and treatment—the finest etched portrait that has been wrought by any one since the very masterpieces of Rembrandt, nor, honestly speaking, do I know that it fails to stand comparison even with these.

Like his most prolific and perhaps also his most original pupil, who has been spoken of already, Legros has little sense of womanly beauty; but the lines of his landscape—often, as I judge, either an imagined world or but a faded memory of our own—have refinement

126

and charm. His art is restful—restful even when it is weird. A large proportion of his earlier work records the life of the priesthood. In its visible dignity—as I have said elsewhere—its true but limited *camaraderie*, in its monotony and quietude, in its magnificence of service and symbol, the life of the priest, and of those who serve in a great church, has impressed Legros profoundly; and he has etched these men—one now reading a lesson, one waiting now with folded hands, one meditating, one observant, one offering up the Host, another, a musician, bending over the 'cello or the double-bass with slow movement of the hand that holds the bow. Dignity and ignorance, pomp and power, weariness, senility, decay—none of these things escape the observation of the first great etcher of the life of the Church. *Communion dans l'Eglise St. Médard* and *Chantres Espagnols*, when seen in fine " states," are amazing and admirable technical triumphs, as well as penetrating studies, the one of religious fervour, the other of impending death. In *La Mort et le Bûcheron* —in either version of the plate, for there are two— the imagination of Legros is at its tenderest. Is not *L'Incendie* dramatic, in its large and abstract way? Is not *La Mort du Vagabond*—with the storm like the storm in " Lear "—the one *very* large etching that is not, in its scale, a mistake? I know I would not have it otherwise, though it wants almost a portfolio to itself, or, better, a frame upon the wall. One might go on indefinitely; but again it is preferable to send the reader to the study of the master's long and serious

work—a hundred and sixty-eight pieces there were in
1877, when Thibaudeau & Malassis published their Catalogue; ten years later there were ninety additions to the
list; and to this day Mr. Legros has not ceased to etch.
Only the very first of his prints show any evidence
of technical incompleteness. The very latest—though
no doubt, by this time, his own real message must have
been delivered—the very latest show no symptom of
fatigue or of decay.

Not more than once or twice, I think, in all his long
career, has Legros published his works in sets, either
naturally connected or artificially brought together.
Charles Holroyd, a distinguished pupil of Legros's, has
twice already published sets—there is his "Icarus"
set, and a little earlier in date, yet in no respect immature, his "Monte Oliveto" set. Holroyd—with individuality of his own, without a doubt—is yet Legros's
true spiritual child. He has much of his refinement,
of his dignity. Did he love the priesthood from
Legros's etchings, before ever he lived with them in
Italy? Rome itself, I suppose, gave him the love of
what is visibly Classic—and that is a love which Legros
does not appear to share. His composition is generally
admirable; his sense of beautiful "line" most noteworthy. His trees — stone pine and olive, or the
humbler trees of our North—are thus not only individual studies, true to Nature sometimes in detail,
always in essentials—but likewise restful and impressive decorations of the space of paper it is his business
to fill. *Farm behind Scarborough* shows him homely,

simple, and direct. Was it a Roman garden, or Studley, that suggested *The Round Temple?* In the little plate of the *Borghese Gardens*—my own private plate, which I bought from him when the first impression of it hung at the Painter-Etchers' five or six years ago—Holroyd consciously abandons much that is wont to attract (atmospheric effect, for example), but he retains the thing for which the plate existed—dignified and expressive rhythm of " line." That justifies it, and permits it to omit much, and to only exquisitely hint at the thing it would not actually convey.

We will turn for a few minutes to another contemporary who has etched in the right spirit—Mr. Frank Short. Some people think that Mr. Short has not quite fulfilled the promise which only a few years ago he gave, as an original etcher. For myself, I consider that the fulfilment is, at most, only delayed : not rendered unlikely. Mr. Short has been for several years extremely busy in the translation, chiefly into mezzotint, of pictures and drawings by artists as various as Turner, Nasmyth, Constable, Dewint, and G. F. Watts. If engravings that are not original inventions are ever worth buying—and that, of course, cannot be doubted—these translations by Mr. Short are worth buying, eminently. There is not one of them that fails. His flexibility is extraordinary. His productions are exquisite. In a parenthesis, let me advise their purchase, when things of the sort are required. But Short is before us just now only in the capacity of an original etcher, and, as an original etcher, with well-nigh per-feet command of *technique*, he registers the daintiest of individual impressions of the world. That his field as an observer at first hand is limited, is certainly true. Coast subjects please him best. We have no finer draughtsman of low-lying land, of a scene with a low horizon, of a great expanse of mud and harbour deserted by the tide—all their simplicity, even uncomeliness of theme, made almost poetic. *Low Tide and the Evening Star ; Evening, Bosham ; Sleeping till the Flood*, are all, among subjects of this order, prints that should be secured where it is possible—and where the accumulation of modern etchings is not an inconvenience. In *Stourbridge Canal* and in *Wrought Nails* —both of them finely felt, finely drawn bits of the ragged, sordid "Black Country"—we have desirable instances of Mr. Short's dealings with another class of theme. If you want him in a more playful mood, take *Quarter Boys*—a quite imaginative yet gamesome vision of urchins looking out to sea from the Belfry of the church of Rye.

C. J. Watson has for many years now been etching persistently, and been etching well. But he has not got, and could not perhaps quite easily get, beyond the learned simplicity of *Mill Bridge, Bosham*, done in 1888. It is a sketch with singular unity of impression —or rather with that unity of impression which is not so singular perhaps when the work remains a sketch. *St. Etienne-du-Mont*—a theme from which one would have thought that Mr. Watson would have been warned off, remembering how, once and for ever, it had been

130

dealt with by the genius of Méryon—is, doubtless, an accurate enough portrait, but the individuality—where? And without individuality, such work is an architectural drawing. This *St. Etienne* bears date 1890; but since 1890 Mr. Watson has done finer things—his strong and capable hand stirred to expression by a nature not perhaps very sensitive to every effect of beauty, but feeling the interest of solid workmanship and something of the charm of the picturesque. *Ponte del Cavallo* has daintiness, and some yet more recent work in Central Italy and Sicily—with architecture generally as the basis of its interest—may fall reasonably enough within the province of collectors who can afford to accumulate—who can afford to add well to well and vineyard to vineyard.

Of the remaining English etchers of our time, Colonel Goff, Mr. D. Y. Cameron, and Mr. Oliver Hall are those whom it will be best to notice. Mr. Macbeth, Mr. Herkomer, Mr. Pennell, Mr. W. H. May, Mr. Mempes, Mr. Raven Hill, Mr. Haig, Miss Bolingbroke, Mrs. Stanhope Forbes—others besides—have brought out prints of which the possession is pleasant; but it is, I suppose, the three men whom I named earlier who by reason of combined quality and quantity of "output" most deserve the collector's serious consideration.

Of these three, Goff—a retired Guardsman, but no more really an amateur than Seymour Haden—is, I take it, the best known. Actual popularity he has been, for an etcher, wonderfully near to attaining. He may even now attain it. Much of the excellence

131

of his work is easily intelligible; his point of view, though always artistic, is one that can be reached, often, by the ordinary spectator of his prints. Hence, his relatively large acceptance—an agreeable circumstance which I should be glad to consider was owing exclusively to the skill that is certainly likewise his. Colonel Goff's sympathies are broad; his subjects admirably varied; and the vivacity of his artistic temperament allows him to attack each new plate with new interest. He is almost without mannerism in treatment, and of that which presents itself to his gaze on his journey through the world, there is singularly little which he is not able artistically to tackle. Not quite the architectural draughtsman that C. J. Watson is, he yet can indicate tastefully the architecture of church or cottage or city house. His sympathies are with the new as much as with the old, and that is in part because to him a building is not only, or chiefly, a monument with historical associations; it is, above all, an excuse and a justification for an arrangement on the copper, of harmonious and intricate line. Very successfully he has dealt with landscape. Is it the seaboard or the town that he depicts, he can people the place with figures vivacious and rightly displayed. I suppose that he has executed by this time scarcely less than a hundred plates. *Summer Storm in the Itchen Valley* remains the most popular, and would therefore prove, in an auction-room, the least inexpensive. But, among the pure etchings, *Pine Trees, Christ Church*, and *Norfolk Bridge, Shore-*

132

ham, and the extremely delicate little print of the *Chain Pier, Brighton,* and *Low Tide, Mouth of the Hampshire Avon*—with its own dreary but impressive beauty—are to my mind distinctly more desirable, and should be possessed if possible; whilst among the dry-points (and a dry-point can never be common) I would place highest, perhaps, the peaceful little *Itchen Abbas Bridge.*

Intricate in arrangement of line, the work of Colonel Goff is in actual workmanship less elaborate than that of Mr. D. Y. Cameron, who, though now and again, as in that which remains almost his masterpiece—*Border Towers*—a pure sketcher in Etching, much oftener devotes himself to work solid, substantial, deliberate rather in fulness of realisation than in economy of means. He is a fine engraver on the copper; addicted to massive arrangements of shadow and light—giving to these, wherever there is any fair excuse for doing so, a little of the Celtic weirdness Mr. Strang bestows upon the figure. Glamour, just a touch of wizardy, is in the *Palace, Stirling Castle;* and not in that only. A master, already, of the arrangement of light and shade—a master, already, of *technique*—Mr. Cameron (who has studied Rembrandt so much, and, I should presume, Méryon) is finding his own path. Indeed, the *Border Towers* shows that all that he has learnt from Rembrandt he has made his own by this time. How else could he have accomplished what is certainly one of the most complete and significant suggestions of Landscape wrought in our day! A *Rembrandt Farm* is earlier. It is extremely clever, but, as its very name might lead one to conjecture, it is more distinctly imitative. Mr. Cameron was not a master at the moment when he wrought the *Flower Market*, because if he did not make in that the irremediable mistake of choosing the wrong medium—printer's ink where one's cry, first and last, is naturally for "colour"—he made at all events the mistake that Mr. Whistler is incapable of making (as his etching of *The Garden* shows), the mistake of working with a heavy hand, when what was wanted was a treatment of "touch and go," as it were—the very lightest coquetry of line. Occasionally Mr. Cameron has failed; occasionally his industry has resulted in the commonplace; but he is a young man still; the collector must take account of him; his may hereafter be a very distinguished name; and meanwhile—now even—the collector of good Modern Etching is bound to put into his folios a few of Mr. Cameron's always sterling prints.

Mr. Oliver Hall—a young man also, and one who paints in water-colour as well as etches—can hardly have done as many plates as Mr. Cameron, yet; and in none of them, free sketches of landscape—breezy, immediate, well-disposed—has Mr. Hall been so unwise as to emulate the almost Méryon-like elaboration not inappropriate to at all events the architectural subjects of Cameron. Oliver Hall's is delightful and masculine work. After a very short period of immaturity, during which the influence of Seymour Haden was that which he most disclosed, his *Trees on the Hillside* and *A Windy Day* testified to an extraordinary flexibility and force. The lines of "foliage," as people call it—it is the tree, however, rather than the leaf—the lines of the tree-form, however intricate, did not elude his point. Afterwards, *Angerton Moss: Windy Day*, and the *Edge of the Forest*, with its gust-blown trees and threatening sky, and later still, *King's Lynn from a Distance*, came to assure us that here was an artist getting at the heart of Nature—a master who could bring before us a broad poetic vision of natural effects.

Mr. Alfred East, Mr. Mempes, Mr. Jacomb Hood, Mr. Percy Thomas, Mr. J. P. Heseltine, Mr. W. H. May, Sir Charles Robinson, Elizabeth Armstrong (Mrs. Stanhope Forbes), and Minna Bolingbroke (Mrs. C. J. Watson) ought not to go unmentioned even in a book which has a wider field than "Etching in England"—in which some of them are named less baldly.

The inexpert purchaser may like to know what is the sort of price asked generally by its producer, or by the dealer, or the Painter-Etchers' Society—to which the print may be intrusted—for a new etching. I am here on ticklish ground; but I must make bold to answer, speaking broadly, "Far too much." Later on—before I have quite done with the subject of the Litho-graph—I shall return to the charge, on this matter of solid cash. But each class of work stands, in the matter of price, on its own peculiar footing; and here we talk, not of lithographs, but of etchings and dry-points. The wholly exceptional genius, approved by Time, and happily yet with us to benefit by the result of his fame, may be pardoned for asking twelve

guineas for one of his most recent etchings. If he
gets it, his rewards are delightfully contrasted with
those of Méryon — who was grateful when an old
gentleman in the French War Office gave him a franc
and a half for an impression of the *Abside de Notre
Dame*, which, because of its beauty and of its peculiar
and rare " state," is worth to-day about a hundred and
fifty pounds. But we are not all men of exceptional
genius; and, in the case of etched work, which, without
deterioration, may be issued to the number of fifty or
a hundred or a couple of hundred impressions, is it
wise to seek to anticipate what after all may prove not
to be the verdict of the world ?— is it wise to limit the
issue so very artificially by the simple, I will not say
the greedy process of asking two, three, and four
guineas for an impression of a good but ordinary etching ? A good etching, produced by a contemporary
artist, could, quite to the benefit of the etcher, be sold
for a guinea. If the etcher has not time to print it
himself, or is not, at heart, artist enough to wish to do
so, let him send it to a good printer, with definite in-
structions how to print it, and, on the average, each
impression may cost him half-a-crown. Then, of course,
if he sells it through a dealer, there will be something
for the dealer—perhaps five shillings. Say about four-
teen shillings will be left for the artist. The fee is
insignificant—but, if you once interest the public, it
may be almost indefinitely multiplied. The price that
is prohibitive to the ordinary man of taste—the price
that prevents him, not, of course, from buying an

etching here and there, but from forming any considerable collection of etchings—that, if the artist only knew it, is the greatest possible disadvantage to himself. He is concerned for his dignity; his *amour-propre*, he sometimes says. But an etching—like a book—is a printed thing; and the author of a book conceives, and rightly, that his *amour-propre* is wounded rather by absence or narrow restriction of sale than by the moderation—the lowness, if you will—of the price at which his book is issued.

Now a dry-point and an ordinary etching stand on different ground in this respect. Both are printed things, indeed; but whilst the etching will, according to its degree of force or delicacy, yield, without "steeling," from fifty to four hundred impressions — and generally quite as near the four hundred as the fifty— a dry-point will inevitably deteriorate after a dozen or twenty impressions, and may even deteriorate after three or four. Each impression, then, of a dry-point that is desirable at all, has its own peculiar value—its rarity to begin with (unless you work it to death), and its unlikeness to its neighbour. I blame no good artist, when he has made a good dry-point, for asking two or three or four, or six or seven, guineas for it. I do not as work of art—as providing me with joy—esteem it any more highly than the etching. The etching, which I ought to acquire at a guinea, may give me the gratification of a Wordsworthian poem. It may be—happy chance for every one concerned if it is!—as directly inspired as the *Ancient Mariner:* it may be a thing conceived and wrought in one of those "states of the atmosphere" which (it is Coleridge himself who says it) are "addressed to the soul." Do I underrate it? Not a jot. But I discern that, like the *Ancient Mariner*, it can be multiplied in large numbers. The dry-point cannot.

Even at the risk of being charged with a certain repetition of my argument, I shall return—as the reader has been warned already—it will be somewhere in the chapter on modern Lithography—to this question of the too extravagant price, and therefore of the necessarily too restricted sale, of the contemporary print.

CHAPTER VII

Recent Interest in Martin Schöngauer — A graceful Primitive—Dürer the exponent of the fuller Renaissance — Some principal Dürers—Their prices at the Fisher Sale—German "Little Masters"—The Ornament of Aldegrever — The range of the Behams—Altdorfer — Other Little Masters — And Lucas Van Leyden.

AMONG the least reprehensible, and also among the least widely diffused, of the recent fads of the collector, there is to be reckoned a certain increase in the consideration accorded to the work of Martin Schöngauer. If Martin Schöngauer's ingenious and engaging plates —naïve in conception, and, in execution, dainty—came ever to be actually preferred to the innumerable pieces which attest the potency and the variety of Dürer, that preference might possibly be explained, but could never be justified. As it is, however, no reasonable admirer of "the great Albert" can begrudge to one who was after all to some extent his predecessor, and not in all things his inferior, the honourable place which, after many generations of comparative neglect, that predecessor has lately taken, and now seems likely to hold. Schöngauer, even more it may be than Albert Dürer himself, was, as it were, a path-breaker. The interest of the Primitive belongs to him ; and the interest of

139

the simple. Some of his religious conceptions were expressed in prettier form—and form on that account more readily welcomed—than any that was taken on by the conceptions of the giant mind that even now draws us upon our pilgrimage to Nuremberg, as Goethe draws us to Weimar. The Virgin of Schöngauer is more acceptable to the senses than the average Virgin of Dürer, whose children, on the other hand (see especially the delightful little print, *The Three Genii*, Bartsch 66), have the larger lines and lustier life of the full Renaissance. A touch of what appeals to us as a younger naïveté, and a touch of what appeals to us as elegance, are especially discernible in the earlier artist's work; and that work too, or much of it, has often the additional attractiveness of exceptional scarcity. Likewise, it is to most of us less familiar. But when all these elements of attraction have been allowed for, the genius of Albert Dürer—so much deeper and so much broader, at once more philosophical and more dramatic, and expressed by a craftsmanship so much more changeful and more masterly — the genius of Albert Dürer dominates. If our allegiance has wavered, if we have been led astray for a period, by Martin Schöngauer himself, it may be, or by somebody less worthily illustrious, we shall return, wearily wise, to the author of the *Melancholia* and the *Nativity*, of the *Knight of Death* and of *The Virgin by the City Wall*. To study long and closely the work of the original engravers, is to come, sooner or later, quite certainly to the conclusion that there are two artists standing above all the

rest, and that it was theirs, pre-eminently, to express, in the greatest manner, the greatest mind. One of these two artists, of course, is Rembrandt. And the other is Dürer.

Adam Bartsch, working at Vienna, in the beginning of this century, upon those monumental books of reference which, as authorities upon their wide subject, are even now only partially displaced, catalogued about a hundred and eight metal plates as Albert Dürer's contribution to the sum of original engraving. The Rev. C. H. Middleton-Wake, working in 1893—and profiting by the investigations, all of them more or less recent, of Passavant and G. W. Reid, of Thausing, Dürer's biographer, and Mr. Koehler, the Keeper of the Prints at Boston, Massachusetts—has catalogued one hundred and three. The number — not so considerable as Schöngauer's, by about a couple of score— does not, at first thought, seem enormous for one the greater portion of whose life was given to original engraving; but then, it must be remembered, Dürer's life, though not exactly a short, was scarcely a long one. And, again, whatever may have been the processes he employed, and even if, as Mr. Middleton-Wake supposes, etched work, as well as burin-work, helped him greatly along his way, the elaboration of his labour was never lessened; the order of completeness he strove for and attained had nothing in common with the completeness of the sketch. His German pertinacity and dogged joy in work for mere work's sake, never permitted him to dismiss an endeavour until he had carried it to actual realisation. Each piece of his is not so much a page as a volume. The creations of his art have the lastingness and the finality of a consummate Literature, and of those three material things with which such Literature has been compared—

"*marbre, onyx, émail,*"—

as the phrase goes, of one who wrought on phrases as Cellini on the golden vase, and Dürer on the little sheet of burnished copper.

Of the hundred and three prints which, in the Fitz-William Museum, Mr. Middleton-Wake placed in what he believes to be their chronological order—many, of course, their author himself dated, but many afford room for the exercise of critical ingenuity and care—sixteen belong to the series known as "The Passion upon Copper," which is distinguished by that title from the series of seven-and-thirty woodcuts known generally as "The Little Passion." The "Passion upon Copper," executed between the year 1507 and the year 1513, are pronounced "unequal in their execution," "not comparing favourably with Dürer's finer prints," and "engraved for purposes of sale." Now most of Dürer's work was "engraved for purposes of sale"—that is, it was meant to be sold—but what the critic may be supposed to mean, in this case, is, that the designs were due to no inspiration; the execution, to no keen desire. Four much later pieces—including two *St. Christophers*—are spoken of with similar disparagement. I am

142

unable to perceive the justice of the reproach when it
is applied to the *Virgin with the Child in Swaddling
Clothes*—a print of which it is remarked that it, like
certain others, is "without any particular charm or
dignity ; being taken quite casually from burgher-life,
and only remarkable for the soft tone of the engraving."
No doubt the *Virgin with the Child in Swaddling Clothes*
is inspired by the human life—and that was "burgher-
life" necessarily—which Dürer beheld ; and it is none
the worse for that. It is not one of the very finest of
the Virgins, but it is simple, natural, healthy, and it is
characteristic, as I seem to see, not only in its *technique*,
but in its conception. What more fascinating than the
little bit of background, lavished there, so small and yet
so telling ?—a little stretch of shore, with a town placed
on it, and great calm water : a reminiscence, it may be,
of Italy—a *décor* from Venice—a bit of distance too
recalling the distance in the *Melancholia* itself. But we
must pass on, to consider briefly two or three points in
Dürer's work : points which we shall the better illus-
trate by reference to the greater masterpieces.

The year 1497 was reached before the master of
Nuremberg affixed a date to any one of his plates.
That is the not quite satisfactory composition, curiously
ugly in the particular realism it affects—and yet, in a
measure, interesting—*A Group of Four Naked Women*.
Thausing doubts, or does more than doubt, the originality of the design. Mr. Middleton-Wake holds that
in execution, at least, it shows distinct advance upon
Dürer's earlier work, and amongst earlier work he in-

cludes no less than three-and-twenty of the undated plates: putting the *Ravisher* first, with 1494 as its probable year, and putting last before the *Group of Naked Women*, a piece which he maintains to be the finest of the earlier prints, the *Virgin and Child with the Monkey*.

Looking along the whole line of Dürer prints, in what he deems to be their proper sequence, Mr. Middleton-Wake observes, as all observe indeed, wonderful variations—differences in execution so marked that at first one might hesitate to assign to the same master, pieces wrought so differently. He argues fully how their dissimilarity is due "either to a marked progression in their handling" or to an alteration in their actual method. For quick perception of such partly voluntary change, the student is referred to an examination of the *Coat of Arms with the Skull*, the *Coat of Arms with the Cock*, the *Adam and Eve*, the *St. Jerome*, and the *Melancholia*. The year 1503 was probably the date of the two Coats of Arms; the great print of the *Adam and Eve* carries its date of "1504"; the *St. Jerome* is of 1512; the *Melancholia* of 1514. The practical point established for the collector by such differences as are here visible, and which a study of these particular examples by no means exhausts, is that he must most carefully avoid the not unnatural error of judging an impression of a Dürer print by its attainment or its non-attainment of the standard established by some other Dürer print he knows familiarly already. The aims technically were so very different, he must know each print to say with any certainty—save in a few most obvious cases—whether a given impression, that seems good, is, or is not, desirable. The "silver-grey tone," for example, so charming in one print, may be unattainable in, or unsuitable to, another.

Upon the question of the meaning of certain prints of Dürer, any amount of ingenious, interesting conjecture has been expended in the Past. One of Mr. Stopford Brooke's sermons—I heard it preached, now many years ago, in York Street—is a delightful essay on the *Melancholia*. For suggestions as to the allegorical meaning of *The Knight of Death*, it may be enough to refer the reader to Thausing (vol. ii. page 225) and to Mrs. Heaton's Life of Dürer (page 168). The *Jealousy*, Dürer speaks of, in his Netherlands Diary, as a "Hercules." *The Knight and the Lady*, Thausing says, is one of those Dance of Death pictures so common in the Middle Age. Of the *Great Fortune*, Thausing holds that its enigmatical design, with the landscape below, has direct reference to the Swiss War of 1499, and this we may agree with; but, explaining, it may be, too far, he writes in detail, "The winged Goddess of Justice and Retribution stands, smiling, on a globe; carrying in one hand a bridle and a curb for the too presumptuous fortunate ones; in the other, a goblet for unappreciated worth." Mr. Middleton-Wake, wisely less philosophical, urges a simpler meaning. The city of Nuremberg, he reminds us, had, in compliance with Maximilian's demand, furnished four hundred foot soldiers and sixty horse, for the campaign in Switzerland, and at the head of these troops was Pirkheimer, to whom on his return his fellow-citizens offered a golden cup. " We assume," says Mr. Middleton-Wake, " that it is this cup which Dürer places in the hand of the Goddess." With the Swiss War are also associated the *Coat of Arms with the Cock* and the even rarer (certainly not finer) *Coat of Arms with a Skull.* The one may symbolise the anticipated success, the other the failure, of the campaign into Switzerland.

A reference to the Richard Fisher Sale Catalogue (at Sotheby's, May 1892) affords as ready and as correct a means as we are likely to obtain of estimating the present value of fine Dürer prints. Mr. Fisher's collection was unequal ; but it was celebrated, and it was, on the whole, admirable. It was, moreover, practically complete, and in this way alone it represented an extraordinary achievement in Collecting. Its greatest feature was Mr. Fisher's possession of the *Adam and Eve* in a condition of exceptional brilliancy, and with a long pedigree, from the John Barnard, Maberly, and Hawkins collections. This was the first Albert Dürer that passed under the hammer on the occasion, and so opened the sale of the Dürers with a thunderclap, as it were—Herr Meder paying £410 to bear it off in triumph. Then came the *Nativity*, the charming dainty little print, which Dürer himself speaks of as the " Christmas Day." Mr. Gutekunst gave £49 for it. A fine impression of the *Virgin with Long Hair* fetched £51 ; an indifferent one of the more beautiful

146

Virgin seated by a Wall, £10, 15s. The *St. Hubert*
sold for £48—a finer impression of the same subject
selling, in the Holford Sale, just a year later, for £150
—the *Melancholia*, £39; but, it must be remembered,
the *Melancholia*, though always one of the most sought
for, is not by any means one of the rarest Dürers. The
Knight of Death passed, for £100, into the hands of
Mr. Gutekunst. An early impression of the *Coat of
Arms with the Cock* was bought by Mr. Kennedy for
£20; the *Coat of Arms with the Skull* going to Messrs.
Colnaghi for £42. In the Holford Sale a yet finer
impression of this last subject was bought by Herr
Meder for £75.

Before I leave, for a while at least, the prosaic questions of the Sale-Room, and pass on to direct attention
to the artistic virtues of the " Little Masters," let the
" beginning collector," as the quaint phrase runs, be
warned in regard to copies. It has not been left for an
age that imitates everything—that copies our charming
Battersea Enamel, *tant bien que mal*, and the " scale-
blue " of old Worcester, and the lustre of Oriental—it
has not been left for such an age to be the first to copy
Dürer. In fact, no one now-a-days bestows the labour
required in copying Dürer. He is copied now-a-days
only in the craft of *photogravure*. But, of old time,
Wierix, and less celebrated men, copied him greatly.
This is a matter of which the collector—at first at
least—has need to beware. It must be stamped upon
his mind that Dürer's work at a certain period did
much engage the copyist. It engaged the copyist only

less perhaps than did the work of Rembrandt himself, through successive generations.

And now we speak, though briefly, of the seven German "Little Masters," of whom the best are never "little" in style, but, rather, great and pregnant, richly charged with quality and meaning: "little" only in the mere scale of their labour. The print-buyer who is in that rudimentary condition that he only considers the walls of his sitting-rooms, and buys almost exclusively for their effective decoration, does not look at the Little Masters. Upon a distant wall, their works make little spots. But in a corner, near the fire—on the right-hand side of that arm-chair in which you seek to establish your most cossetted guest, the person (of the opposite sex, generally) whom you are glad to behold—a little frame containing half-a-dozen Behams, Aldegrevers, to be looked at closely (pieces of Ornament perhaps ; exercises in exquisite l. e), adds charm to an interior which, under circumst. nces of Romance, may need indeed no added charm at all from the mere possessions of the collector. Still—there are moods. And if the German Little Masters come in pleasantly enough, on an odd foot or so of wall, now and then, how justified is their presence in the port-folio—in the solander box—when the collector is really a serious one, and when he no longer bestows upon living, breathing Humanity all the solicitude that was meant for his Behams!

To talk more gravely, the German Little Masters should indeed be collected far more widely than they are, amongst us. Scarcely anything in their appeal is particular and local. Their qualities—the qualities of the best of them—are exquisite and sterling, and are for all Time.

The seven Little Masters, on whom the late Mr. W. Bell Scott—one of the first people here in England to collect them—wrote, in an inadequate series, one of the few quite satisfactory books, are, Altdorfer, Barthel Beham, Sebald Beham, Aldegrever, Pencz, Jacob Binck, and Hans Brosamer. One or two of these may quickly be discerned to be inferior to the others; one or two to be superior; but it would be priggish to attempt to range them in definite order of merit. It may suffice to say that to me at least Aldegrever and the Behams appeal most as men to be collected. The Behams—Sebald especially—was a very fine Ornamentist. Aldegrever, it may be, was an Ornamentist yet more faultless. Some examples of his Ornament, the collector should certainly possess. And then he will come back very probably to the Behams, recognising in these two brothers a larger range than Aldegrever had, and a spirit more dramatic—an entrance more vivid and personal into human life, a keen interest in human story. They were realists, not without a touch of the ideal. And in design and execution, they were consummate artists, and not only—which they were too, of course—infinitely laborious and exquisite craftsmen.

Adam Bartsch has catalogued, in his industrious way, according to the best lights of his period, the works of the Little Masters. His volumes are the foundation of all subsequent study. To Altdorfer he assigns ninety-six pieces (I speak of course here, and in every case, of pieces engraved on metal); to Barthel Beham, sixty-four; to Sebald Beham — whose life, though not a long, was yet a longer one than Barthel's — two hundred and fifty-nine; to Jacob Binck, ninety-seven; to George Pencz, a hundred and twenty-six; to Heinrich Aldegrever, no less than two hundred and eighty-nine; to Brosamer, four-and-twenty. But of late years, as was to be expected, certain of these masters have been the subjects of particular study. Thus we have, in England, the dainty little catalogue of Sebald Beham, by the Rev. W. J. Loftie—a book delightfully printed in a very limited edition. That book brings up the number of Sebald Beham's assured plates to two hundred and seventy-four. Dr. Rosenberg has also, in much detail, written in German upon the plates of this fascinating artist; and still more lately M. Edouard Aumüller has published, at Munich, in the French tongue, elaborate, though indeed scarcely final, studies of the Behams and of Jacob Binck.

Of the German Little Masters, Albrecht Altdorfer is the earliest. He was only nine years Dürer's junior; nearly twenty years separate him from others of the group. Born it really even at the present moment seems difficult to say where, Altdorfer, Dr. Rosenberg considers, was actually a pupil of Dürer's—an apprentice, an inmate of his house, probably, soon after Dürer as a quite young man, already prosperous and busy,

150

took up his abode, with his bride, Agnes Frey, at the large house by the Thiergarten Gate. But whatever was the place of Altdorfer's birth and whatever the place of his pupilage—and neither matter, as it seems, is settled conclusively—Ratisbon is the city in which his life was chiefly spent. There he was architect as well as painter and engraver; an official post was given him; and during the last decade of his career his architectural work for Ratisbon caused, it is to be presumed, the complete cessation of his work of an engraver. Merits Altdorfer of course has—variety and ingenuity amongst them—or his fame would hardly have survived; but Mr. W. B. Scott, whose criticism of him was that of an artist naturally rather in sympathy with the methods of his endeavour, never rises to enthusiasm in his account of him. His drawing is not found worthy of any warm commendation, nor his craftsmanship with the copper. The great lessons he might have learnt from Dürer, he does not seem fully to have appropriated. His design is deemed more fantastic. But his range was not narrow, and apart from his practice in what is strictly line-engraving, he executed etchings of Landscape—caring more than Dürer did, perhaps, for Landscape for its own sake: studying it indeed less lovingly in detail, but with a certain then unusual reliance on the interest of its general effect. Some measure of romantic character belongs to his Landscape: "partly intensified," says Mr. Scott, "and partly destroyed, by the eccentric taste that appears in nearly everything from his hand."

151

The pine had fascination for him. "And he loaded its boughs with fronds, like the feathers of birds, and added long lines, vagaries of lines, that have little or no foundation in Nature."

Of both the Behams, Mr. Loftie assures us that they were pupils of Dürer. Greater even than the artist I have just been writing about, they show, it seems to me, at once an influence more direct from Dürer, and an individuality more potent, of their own. Barthel, the younger of the two brothers—one whose designs Sebald, with all his gifts, was not too proud to now and then copy—was born at Nuremberg in 1502. "Le dessin de ses estampes," writes M. Aumüller, "est savant et gracieux, et son burin est d'une élégance brillante et moelleuse." The words—though it is impossible, in a line or two, to generalise a great personality—are not badly chosen. Exiled from Nuremberg, whilst still young, Barthel Beham laboured at Frankfort, and, later, in Italy—a circumstance which accounts for something in the character of his work. For, in Barthel, the Italian influence is unmistakable; he is, as Mr. Scott says truly, "emancipated from the wilful despising of the graces." In Italy, in 1540, Barthel died.

Sebald Beham, the more prolific brother, whose years, ere they were ended, numbered half a century, was born in 1500. He remained at home—not indeed at Nuremberg, but long at Frankfort—yet, remaining at home, his work was somehow more varied. A classical subject one day, and peasant life the next, an

ornament now, and now a design symbolical like his
Melancholia—these interested him in turn; and, as for
his technical achievement, his *Coat of Arms with the
Cock* (for he, like Dürer, had that, as well as a *Melancholia*) would suffice to show, had he nothing else to
show, his unsurpassable fineness of detail. "Cette
superbe gravure," M. Aumüller says—and most justifiably, for technical excellence cannot go any further,
nor is there wanting majesty of Style. At the Loftie
Sale some happy person acquired for £4 this lovely
little masterpiece: at the Durazzo Sale, £5 was the
price of it. Analysis of Sebald Beham's prints shows
that of his noble work on metal seventy-five subjects
are suggested by sacred and nineteen by "profane"
history. Mythology claims thirty-eight designs, and
Allegory thirty-four. Genre subjects, treated with the
various qualities of observation, humour, warmth, ab-
sorb some seventy plates. Of vignettes and ornaments,
there are about two score.

In 1881—several years after he had finished his
Catalogue—the Rev. W. J. Loftie sold in Germany his
remarkable collection of Sebald Beham's works. Next
perhaps, in importance, in recent times, to Mr. Loftie's
collection, was that of Richard Fisher—dispersed at
a sale I have already spoken of. From the Fisher
Sale, which was so comprehensive in its character,
we will take note of the prices here in England of at
least a few fine things—premising that whatever be the
prices fetched by an exceptional rarity, a very few
pounds (often only three or four), spent carefully, will

buy, at a good dealer's, a fine Beham. In the Fisher Sale then, the *Madonna and Child with the Parrot* fetched £5, 10s.; the *Madonna with the Sleeping Child,* £17, 10s. (Meder): the *Venus and Cupid,* £3, 10s. (Deprez); the magnificently drawn *Leda,* only eleven shillings—but then it must have been a bad impression, for a fine one at the Loftie Sale fetched £4, 10s., and at the Kalle Sale, £6—*Death Surprising a Woman in her Sleep,* £3, 12s. (Meder); the *Buffoon and the Two Couples,* £5; the *Two Buffoons,* First State, £7, 12s. (Deprez); the *Ornament with a Cuirass and the two Cupids,* £3, 10s. At the same sale, Aldegrever's *Virgin Sitting* had gone for £7, 10s., and Barthel Beham's *Lucretia* for £4, his *Fight for the Standard* for £4, his *Vignette with Four Cupids* for £4, 4s. But it ought perhaps to be remembered that in several cases the representation of the Little Masters in Mr. Fisher's Sale was not good enough to bring the prices which, under favourable circumstances, are wont to be realised by the finest impressions. In regard to Barthel Beham, I will add that the highest price accustomed to be fetched by any print of his, is fetched by his rare, strong portrait of Charles the Fifth. Having said what I have of it, I cannot say that it is undesirable, but it is quite undesirable if it stands alone—for it is exceptional rather than characteristic. In mere size, for one thing. A First State of it has fetched as much as sixty pounds: a Second State averages about twelve.

To Aldegrever—perhaps the very greatest of the

Ornamentists—the most general of recent students of
the School, Dr. Rosenberg, does the least justice. Mr.
Scott, upon the other hand, asserts his position with
strength; nor will it be unprofitable for amateur or
collector if I quote, at some length, what he says.
The Behams, who were great, and Altdorfer, who was
scarcely great, we have—for our present purposes—
done with already. But about the others Mr. Scott
may well be heard. "George Pencz," he reminds us,
"left the Fatherland and subjected himself to Italian
influence, both in manipulation and in invention, while
Brosamer and Jacob Binck are of comparatively little
consequence." I hope—may I say in a parenthesis?—
that Mr. Scott attached great weight to his "comparatively," for otherwise he did the charming work
of Jacob Binck a rude injustice. But to proceed—
"Aldegrever is the most worthy successor to Dürer,
and is the greatest master of invention, with the truest
German traditions of sentiment and romance, as well as
the most prolific ornamentist. He remains all his life
skilfully advancing in the command of his graver, to
which he remains true. Like Lucas of Leyden, he lives
a secluded life, and his miniature prints continue to
issue from his hands with more and more richness and
independence of poetic thought, until we lose sight of
him, dying where he had lived, in the small town of
Soest, without any writer to record the particulars of
his modest life." It may be added that Rosenberg
considers not only that Aldegrever was never under
Dürer's direct tuition—though carrying out the Dürer

155

traditions—but also that he was never in Nuremberg at
all. And, by this means isolating Aldegrever from the
coterie that grew up in the Franconian town, Rosenberg
derives him rather from Lucas van Leyden. To which
Mr. Scott answers, that if Aldegrever never left his
native Westphalia, never even visited Nuremberg and
Augsburg, "he apprehended the movement wonderfully
from a distance, and appropriated as much as he chose
—happily for his works—as much as properly amalga-
mated with his Northern nature."

A great name has passed our lips in discussing this
thing briefly. I wish that there were space here—
that it had been a part of my scheme to treat, not so
utterly inadequately, Lucas van Leyden. But in a
book of this sort—which must seize, so to say, upon
finger-posts, where it can—half of the business is
renunciation, and I renounce, unwillingly, the fair
discussion of the great early Flemish master. Dürer
himself approved of him: gladly exchanged original
prints with Master Lucas of Leyden, who showed
him courtesy on a journey. Numerically the work of
Lucas is not inferior—rather the other way—to Albert
Dürer's. His range of subject was hardly less extensive,
though his range of mind was less vast. In a dramatic
theme, Lucas of Leyden could hold his own with any
one. He had less of unction and of sentiment—less
depth, in fine, very likely. But the great prints of the
Renaissance in the North are not properly represented
in a collector's portfolios, if the work of this master of
various and prolific industry is altogether omitted. His

draughtsmanship, though it improved with Time, was never the searching draughtsmanship of Dürer, indeed, or of one or two of Dürer's followers. Yet it was expressive and spirited. And spirit, vivacity, a certain grace even, are well discovered in the rare work of Lucas in a particular field in which the Behams and Aldegrever triumphed habitually and in which Albert was occasionally great—I mean the field of Ornament. The rare *Panneau d'Ornements* (Bartsch, 164—dated 1528), in scheme of light and shade, in scheme of action, in ingenious, never-wearying symmetry of line, in telling execution, reaches a place near the summit. The collector, when the chance offers, does well to give the six or seven, eight or ten guineas perhaps, which, in some fortunate hour, may be its ransom.

CHAPTER VIII

Earliest Italian Prints—They interest the Antiquary more than the Collector—Nielli—Baccio Baldini—Mantegna and his restless energy—The calm of Zoan Andrea—Campagnola—The Master of the Caduceus—His "Pagan sentiment"—Marc Antonio—His first practice—His art ripest when his prints interpret Raphael—Important Sales of the Italian Prints.

As one of the chief reasons for the composition of the present volume is that the collector, whether a beginner or more advanced, may have ready access to a little book which supplements to some extent, but does not attempt to supersede, any one amongst the labours of earlier students—and which treats often with especial prominence themes which it seems lay scarcely at all within the range of their inquiries—it will hardly be expected that much shall be said here on the various departments of Italian Engraving. Italian Engraving, from the *nielli* of Florentine goldsmiths to the larger method and selected line of Marc Antonio, has for generations occupied the leisure and been the subject of the investigations of many studious men. Volumes have been written about it: treatises,

158

articles, catalogues, correspondence innumerable. About
Italian Engraving—in any one of its branches—it
would be as easy, or as difficult, to say something
new, and at the same time to the point, as it would
be to write with freshness about the decorations of the
Sistine Chapel or such an accepted masterpiece as the
Madonna di San Sisto. The few words I shall write
upon the subject will be of a wholly rudimentary
character. If the reader wishes to go into this subject
elaborately, I refer him at once to experts. No one
is less an expert upon it than I am; but partly that
all sense of balance shall not be wanting to this book,
and partly that the beginner, even with this book
alone, shall not grope wholly in the dark, the place of
the Italians must be briefly recognised. In recognising
it, I do not claim to do more, of my own proper knowledge, than bring to bear upon the question the results
of some more general studies, and perhaps the side-
lights thrown from more particular investigations into
other branches of the engraver's achievement.

The *nielli*—those things wrought so minutely by the
early goldsmiths, Maso da Finiguerra and the rest—
which are the very foundations of Engraving, are, to
begin with, *introuvable*. To the practical collector then,
it cannot be pretended that they appeal, though they
may engage the attention of the student. Then again,
in fine condition, not spoilt by the retouching—nay,
re-working—of the plate, or the wear of the particular
impression through its long life of more than three
hundred years, the somewhat maturer work of the great

Primitives, or of those who, like Mantegna himself, stands, a link upon a borderland, is scarcely within the region of practical commerce. The finer work of the line-engravers upon copper, of the earlier Renaissance in Italy, does not, save on the rarest occasions, appear in Sotheby's auction-room. Perhaps its very scarcity, its gradual absorption during more than one generation, into such great private collections as are not likely to be dispersed, and, yet more, into national, or university, or municipal collections, into which everything entering takes at once, and with no period of novitiate, the black veil—perhaps this very scarcity is accountable for the lack of vivid interest in such work on the part of the collector of modern mind. After all, even masterpieces have their day : much more those things of which it must be said, that though endowed with a great vigour of conception and executed often in trenchant, if not persuasive, form, they do not in execution reach the standards set up for us—and passing now almost into the position of " precedents " —by the later *technique*.

If, of the work of the greatest master of the German Renaissance—of the greatest, most original, most comprehensive mind in the whole of German Art— it is possible to speak as that very fair and penetrating critic, Mr. P. G. Hamerton speaks, in his general essay on Engraving, which appears in the " Encyclopædia Britannica," what is to be said of the earlier Italians? Why, in the very passage in which Mr. Hamerton—far too intelligent, of course, to deny the greatness of his qualities—devotes to Dürer, they, by something more than implication, are to take their share of the dispraise. After telling us that Martin Schöngauer's art is a stride in advance of that of "The Master of 1466," Mr. Hamerton adds, "Outline and shade, in Schöngauer, are not nearly so much separated as in Baccio Baldini, and the shading, generally in curved lines, is far more masterly than the straight shading of Mantegna. Dürer continued Schöngauer's curved shading with increasing manual dexterity and skill; and as he found himself able to perform feats with the burin which amused both himself and his buyers, he overloaded his plates "—"some" of his plates, would here have been a reasonable qualification—"with details, each of which he finished with as much care as if it were the most important thing in the composition." "The engravers of those days "—it is said further—" had no conception of any necessity for subordinating one part of their work to another. In Dürer, all objects are on the same plane." Here Mr. Hamerton generalises too much; but a strong, exaggerated statement on the matter directs at all events our attention to it.

A like criticism could be passed on some, though, it must needs be said, on less, of the Italian work of the earlier time. As a rule, when the pure Primitives had passed, Italian work was less complicated. In Mantegna himself, an immense energy in the figure—the completeness with which the artist was charged with the need of expressing action, and, it may be, the sentiment besides, in which the action had its source—restrained him, stayed his hand, diverted his attention from inappropriate or superfluous detail. And there were other Italian artists of the burin in whom a rising feeling for large and decorative grace had something of the same effect. And when we come to Marc Antonio himself—trained though he was as a copyist of Northern Schools—we see him able, when addressing himself to render the compositions of Raphael, to subordinate everything to the attainment of noble and elegant contour. The finest Marc Antonios—the *Saint Cecilia* and the *Lucretia*, to name but two of them (respectively £25 and £170 in a great Sale three years ago) —were wrought under Raphael's immediate influence; were sculpturesque and simple, never elaborately pictorial—the result, no doubt, in part, of the circumstance that Raphael as well as his engraver recognised that if designs (drawings, not pictures) were the objects of copy, they could be interpreted without going outside the proper art of the engraver. Whatever be the fashions of the moment—and Marc Antonio's prices, notwithstanding an exceptional sum for an exceptional print, are, in the main, low—it must be remembered that, even with his limitations, it was in him and in his School that real pure line-engraving reached maturity. "He retained," says Mr. Hamerton, summarising well enough the situation in a sentence—"he retained much of the early Italian manner in his backgrounds, where its simplicity gives a desirable sobriety ; but his figures are boldly modelled in curved lines, crossing each other in the darker shades, but left single in the passages from dark to light, and breaking away in fine dots as they approach the light itself, which is of pure white paper." As general description, this is excellent; but if the new collector, taking to Marc Antonio, and buying him at a time when, if I may adopt the phraseology of Capel Court, his stock is quoted below par, wishes the opportunity of guidance in the study of the development of his art, let him take up almost the latest book that deals with the subject with minuteness and suggestiveness, if it may not be invariably accurate or systematically arranged —I mean the "Early History of Engraving in North Italy," by the late Richard Fisher, whose name as a collector and connoisseur I do not mention now for the first time. Very interesting too is all that Mr. Fisher has to say about "the Master of the Caduceus," Dürer's friend and instructor, Jacopo de' Barbarj, who, known as Jacob Walsh, was supposed to be German, although practising much at Venice. Passavant, who admits some thirty pieces by him, considers him of German birth—a thing allowed neither by Fisher nor Duplessis. "In single figures"—writes Mr. Fisher— "we have the best illustration of his talent—Judith with the head of Holofernes and a young woman looking at herself in a mirror." At the British Museum a bust portrait of a young woman, catalogued by Bartsch as amongst the anonymous Italians, has been given to Barbarj. M. Galichon considers him eminently Pagan in sentiment. Nor is this incompatible with Richard

Fisher's statement that in style his Holy Families are completely Italian.

"La Gravure en Italie avant Marc Antoine"—a substantial work by Delaborde—is a book that will not pass unnoticed by those whose choice is for the earlier members of the Italian School. Campagnola, it may be—whose chief piece, the *Assumption*, fetched more than £50 at the Durazzo Sale, and whose *Dance of Cupids* reached £50 at the Marochetti—he will find adequately treated there; and there too are made in compact form certain instructive comparisons between Mantegna's work and that of Zoan Andrea and Antonio da Brescia whose labours have their likeness to Mantegna's own. In the rare *Dance of Damsels*—"Dance of Four Women," it ought rather to be, for in at least one of its little-draped figures the gravity and fadedness of middle age is well contrasted with the firm and fresh contour and gay alacrity of youth—Zoan Andrea, whose prints are "généralement préférables" to those of Da Brescia, shows finely not only Mantegna's design, but that something of his own which the great Mantuan's design did not give him. Many people have written well on Mantegna; he provokes people, he stimulates them; and Mr. Sidney Colvin, on the so-called "Mantegna Playing-Cards," has written learnedly as an investigator, giving to designs misnamed and misunderstood their right significance. But it is from Delaborde that I will allow myself to quote one brief passage, which is full at least of personal conviction. What more especially characterises—so he puts it—Andrea Mantegna's en-

graved work, is that it is " un mélange singulier d'ardeur et de patience, de sentiment spontané et d'intentions systématiques : c'est enfin dans l'exécution matérielle, le calme d'une volonté sûre d'elle-même et l'inquiétude d'une main irrité par sa lutte avec le moyen." Zoan Andrea's prints do not present these contrasts. " Tout y résulte d'un travail poursuivi avec une parfaite égalité d'humeur ; tout y respire la même confiance tranquille dans l'autorité des enseignements reçus, le même besoin de s'en tenir aux conquêtes déjà faites et aux traditions déjà consacrées." By Mantegna, about twenty-five accepted plates have reached our time. By Zoan Andrea, a larger number have at least been catalogued, and it is argued by some that the least authentic, as well as the least creditable, are sometimes those which bear his signature.

Did I desire to manufacture " padding," nothing would be easier than for me to extend to a long chapter this summary assemblage of brief and almost incidental notes on the Italian Line-Engraving of the remote Past. But as the subject itself is one to which I have never yet been fortunate enough to devote such a measure of study as might entitle me to claim to be heard when speaking of it, and as the literature of the subject exists in such abundance for the curious, I can afford to be short. It may, however, be of some little interest to the collector, if, before passing on to the discussion of another branch of Print-Collecting in which I have ventured to take my own line, and am willing on all occasions to back my own opinion, we look a little into such records of the Sale-room as throw light upon the changing money values of the engravings by Italian masters.

Mr. Julian Marshall, now with us in his middle age, began collecting when he was so young that his great sale occurred as long ago as 1864. Values have changed since that day, very much. Of his four prints by Mantegna, only one — *The Flagellation* — fetched more than £12. That one reached £21—an early perfect state of *The Entombment* going for £11, 10s., and *Christ Descending into Hell* for £9. Domenico Campagnola's *Descent of the Holy Ghost* then fetched £2, 2s. At the Sykes Sale the same impression had fetched £3; at the Harford, £1, 15s. At the Marochetti Sale in 1868, not a single Mantegna, unless *Christ risen from the Dead*, fetched a price of importance, and this only ten guineas; but among the Marc Antonios the *Adam and Eve in Paradise* sold to Mr. Colnaghi for £136, and *The Massacre of the Innocents* to Mr. Holloway for £40. The *Two Fauns carrying a Child in a Basket*—engraved by Marc Antonio, in his finest manner, after an antique—realised £56, and the *Saint Cecilia* £51. In the Bale Collection, in 1881, the *St. Cecilia* fetched £40, and Mariette's impression of the extraordinarily rare *Dance of Cupids* £241. That was borne off by M. Clément, who was then what M. Bouillon is now — "marchand d'estampes de la Bibliothèque Nationale." In the Holford Sale, twelve years afterwards, Marc Antonio's *Adam and Eve* sold to M. Danlos for £180; the *Massacre of the Innocents*

(from the Lely Collection) to the same dealer for £190; and the *St. Cecilia* and *Lucretia* both to Mr. Gutekunst —the first for £31; the second for £66. The great price fetched by a Marc Antonio at this Sale was, however, that paid for *The Plague*—a print which M. Danlos acquired for £370. Taking note of such a sum, one could hardly believe perhaps that Marc Antonios were not rising; but when a master falls, it is in the minor, not the more eminent pieces—or, at least, in average, not exceptional impressions—that we trace most certainly a decline of value. And, taking the *St. Cecilia* alone—one of the most charming of the subjects, as I have said before, though not one of the rarest—we find, on the three occasions of its sale that I have cited, a high price, one less high, and then again a lower. We find, indeed, comparing the prices that were fetched by two impressions not presumably very different—for both were in great Sales—that in 1893 a *St. Cecilia* brought little more than half of what it brought in 1868. The question now for the collector's judgment, as far as money is concerned, is, Is it safe or unsafe for him to buy at just the present stage of a "falling market"? Have Marc Antonios touched bottom? If he buys them now, will he—in the phrase of sprightly ladies "fluttering" in "South Africans"— will he be "getting in on the ground floor"?

The collector has a right to ask himself these seemingly irreverent questions. Nor will he love Art less, or have an eye less delicate, because he is obliged to ask them. I do not know that the possessions of a

167

prudent collector should — taking things all round— bring him, if he desires to sell, much less than he gave for them. It may be quite enough that as long as he keeps and enjoys them, he shall lose the interest of his money. If, in the interval, the value of his prints happens to increase, so much the better for him —obviously. But he enjoys the things themselves, and can scarcely exact that increase.

CHAPTER IX

French Line-Engravers of the Eighteenth Century render well its original Art—The Prints from Watteau, Lancret, and Pater—Watteau's Characteristics—Chardin's Interiors and Studies of the Bourgeoisie—Success of his Domestic Themes—His Portraits and Still-Life are never rendered—The lasting popularity of Greuze —Boucher Prints at a discount — Fragonard and Baudouin—Larreince and Moreau.

THE Eighteenth Century in France witnessed the rise, the development, and the decay or fall of a great School of Art of which the English public remains, even to this day, all but completely ignorant. The easy seductiveness of the maidens of Greuze, with gleaming eyes and glistening shoulders, has indeed secured in England for a certain side of that artist's work a measure of notice in excess of its real importance; and a succession of accidents and the good taste of two or three connoisseurs out of a hundred—they were men of another generation—have made this country the home and resting-place of some of the best of the pictures and drawings of Watteau. But even Watteau is not to be found within our National Gallery. There Greuze and Lancret—Chardin having but lately joined them with but a single pleasant but inadequate picture —there Greuze and Lancret, seen at least in what is adequate and characteristic, share the task of representing French Art of the period when it was most truly French. They are unequal to the mission. And until some can join them who will fulfil it better, the painted work of the French Eighteenth Century will hardly receive its due.

Fortunately, however, French Eighteenth Century artists fared well at the hands of the line-engravers. Even of a painter who possessed more than many others the charm of colour, it could be said by one of the keenest of his critics that the originality of his work passed successfully from the picture to the print. That is what Denis Diderot wrote of Jean Baptiste Simeon Chardin, and it is true of them all, from Watteau downwards. Theirs was the century of Line-Engraving in France, as it was that of Mezzotint in England. And the practitioners of Line-Engraving and of Mezzotint were something beyond craftsmen. Not only were they artists in their own departments— some of them painted, some of them designed : they were in sympathy with Art and possessed by its spirit. Hence the peculiar excellence of their work with burin or scraper—the high success of labours which their intelligence and flexibility forbade to be simply mechanical.

An Exhibition which at my suggestion the Fine Art Society was good enough to venture on, eleven years ago—but which attracted so little attention from the great public we wanted to engage, that it must some day, I suppose, be repeated—aimed to show those engravings in which, with fullest effect, the line-engravers of the Eighteenth Century rendered the thought and the impression of painters or of draughtsmen who were, in most cases, their contemporaries. Watteau was the first of these painters. The prints after his pictures were chiefly wrought in the years directly following his far too early death. His friend, M. de Julienne, planned and saw closely to the execution of that best monument to Watteau's memory. Cochin and Aveline, Le Bas and Audran, Surugue and Brion, Tardieu and Laurent Cars, worked dexterously or nobly, as the case might be, in perpetuation of the master's dignity and grace. Lancret and Pater were often translated by the same interpreters. Chardin's work was popularised—as far as France is concerned—a very few years after, and with substantially the same effect. Later in the century, some changes which were not all improvements, began to be discernible in the newer plates. The manly method of which Laurent Cars was about the most conspicuous master, yielded a little to the softer practice of the interpreters of Lavreince or to the airy yet not inexact daintiness of the method of the translators of Moreau. The later style of engraving was suited to the later draughtsmanship and painting. Probably indeed it was adopted with a certain consciousness of their needs. Anyhow, not one of the conspicuous figures in the history of French Eighteenth Century Design—except Latour, who practically has not been reproduced at all —can be said to have suffered seriously at the hands of his translators. What French pictorial artists thought and saw and tried to tell, upon their canvases and drawing papers, is, in the main, to be read in the prints after their works. In these prints we may note alike the triumphs and the failures of the real French School. There is no denying its deficiencies. But it is as free from conventionality as the great School of Holland—as independent of tradition—and it is as true to the life that it essays to depict.

Along the whole of the Eighteenth Century—not in France only—Watteau, who lived in it but twenty years, is the dominating master. To put the matter roughly and briefly, he is the inventor of familiar grace in Art. His treatment of the figure had its perceptible influence even upon the beautiful design of Gainsborough; and the way in which he saw his world of men and women dictated a method to his successors in France, down to the revival of the more academic Classicism. Artists—when they have been so comprehensive as to occupy themselves with other people's Art—have known generally that Watteau's name has got to stand among only ten or a dozen of the greatest, but the English amateurs, or rather English picture and print buyers, are still but few who are acquainted with his range and feel the sources of his power. He has not been very popular, because, according to ordinary notions, there is but scanty subject in his designs. The characters in his drama are doing little—they are doing nothing, perhaps. But as the knowledge of what real Art is, extends,

172

and as our sensibility to beauty becomes more refined, we shall ask less, in presence of our pictures, what the people are doing, and shall ask more, what they are. Are they engaging?—we shall want to know. Are they pleasant to live with?

Watteau placed a real humanity in an ideal landscape; but it was still a chosen people that entered into his Promised Land, and the chosen people were ladies of the Court and Theatre, and winning children, and presentable men. His pictures—all the large, elaborate, finely wrought prints after them—are the record of what was in some measure in these people's daily lives, yet it was even more in his own dream. "Toute une création de poëme et de rêve est sortie de sa tête, emplissant son œuvre de l'élégance d'une vie surnaturelle." Through all his art he takes his pleasant company to the selected places of the world, and there is always halcyon weather.

Sometimes it is only the comedians of his day—whose mobile faces Watteau had seen behind the footlights of the stage—who make modest picnic, as in the *Champs Elysées* (the engraving by Tardieu)—find shade as in the *Bosquet de Bacchus* (the engraving by Cochin), or enjoy at leisure the terraced gardens, the vista, the great trees of the *Perspective* (the engraving by Crepy). And sometimes—inhabitants no more of a real world—the persons of his drama prepare, with free bearing, to set out upon long journeys. It is now a pilgrimage to Cythera (*L'Embarquement pour Cythère*, or the *Insula Perjucunda*)—suddenly they have been
173

transported indeed to the "enchanted isle" (Le Bas's drawing of the distant mountains in *L'Ile Enchantée*, is, I may say in an underbreath, a little indefinite and puzzling). In any case the land that Watteau's art has made more beautiful than ordinary Nature, is peopled by a Humanity keenly and finely observed, and portrayed with an unlimited control of vivacious gesture and of subtle expression.

The unremitting study that made not only possible but sure an unvarying success, in themes so manifestly limited, is evidenced best in such collections of Watteau's drawings as that acquired gradually by the British Museum, and that yet finer one inherited by the late Miss James, and now, alas! dispersed. There the complete command of line and character is best of all made clear, and the solid groundwork for success in Watteau's pictures is revealed. Elsewhere—in the "Masters of Genre Painting"—I have found space to explain more fully than can be done in these pages, that however manifestly limited were his habitual themes, his range was really great enough, since—not to speak of the "Elysian Fields"—it covered the landscape and the life of the France he knew. He has drawn beggars as naturally as did Murillo; negroes as fearlessly as Rubens; people of the *bourgeoisie* as faithfully almost as Chardin. And, far from the cut chestnut-trees on whose trimmed straightness there falls in an unbroken mass the level light of his gardens, Watteau draws at need the open and common country, peasants and the soldiery, the baggage-train passing

along the endless roads from some citadel that Vauban
planned. What Watteau saw was the sufficient and
the great foundation of all that he imagined, and his
art's abandonment of the everyday world was to exalt
and to refine, rather than to forget it.

The line-engravings after Watteau—largeish, decorative, vigorous while delicate—remain comparatively inexpensive. A rare impression "before letters" attains,
perhaps, now and then a fancy price; but Time has
very little affected the money value of the impressions
with full title, which, if reasonable care is exercised,
can be secured in fine condition, of such a dealer as
Colnaghi, here in England, and in Paris, of Danlos,
say, or of Bouillon—occupied though they all of
them are, habitually, with more costly things. Often
two or three sovereigns buy you an excellent Watteau,
clean and bright, and not bereft of margin. To have
to give as much as £5 for one, would seem almost
a hardship. And the work of Lancret and Pater—
ingenious, interesting practitioners in Watteau's School
—may be annexed at an expense even less considerable.

Lancret was but a follower of Watteau: Pater was
confessedly a pupil. We shall have to come to Chardin to find in French Art the next man thoroughly
original. And Chardin was a great master. But
Lancret and Pater, though they are but secondary,
are still interesting figures. Neither of them, imitative though they were in varying degrees—neither of
them made any pretensions to their forerunner's inspired reverie. Lancret, as far as his invention was

concerned, was at one time satisfied with a symbolism
that was obvious, not to say bald. At another, as in
the sedate *L'Hiver* (engraved by Le Bas), and the
charming pictures of the games of children, *Le Jeu
de Cache-cache* and *Le Jeu des Quatre Coins* (both
of them engraved by De Larmessin), he was grace-
fully real, without effort at a more remote imagination than the themes of reality in gentle or in middle-
class life exacted. At another time again, he lived
so much in actual things, that he could make the
portraits, not of deep grave men indeed such as the
Bossuets and the Fenelons of the Seventeenth Century,
but of the lighter celebrities of his careless day. That
day was Louis the Fifteenth's—"c'était le beau temps
où Camargo trouvait ses jupes trop longues pour danser
la gargouillade." And Lancret painted Mdlle. Camargo
(and Laurent Cars engraved her), springing to lively
airs. Voltaire had said to her, distinguishing all her
alacrity and fire from the more cautious graces of
Sallé, the mistress of poetic pantomime—Voltaire had
said to her—

> " Les nymphes sautent comme vous,
>   Et les Graces dansent comme elle."

And the truth of the description is attested by Lancret's picture, and by the rosy and vivacious pastel in
Latour's Saint-Quentin Gallery.

Pater, a fellow-townsman of Antoine Watteau's, was
his pupil only in Watteau's later years. At that
time Watteau suffered from an irritability bred of
an exhausting disease and of a yet more exhausting

genius. Master and pupil fell out. But, in his last days of all, Watteau summoned to him the painter who had come from his own town, and in a month, for which the younger artist was ever grateful, Pater was taught more than he had ever been taught before. The pupil had the instinct for prettiness and grace, and in cultivating it Watteau was useful. But there was one thing the master could not teach him—originality. And his record of the engaging trivialities of daily life, where pleasure was most gracious and life most easy, was undertaken by a mind wholly contented with its task. The mind aspired no farther. The faces of Watteau, especially in his studies, are often faces of thoughtful beauty; sometimes, of profound and saddening experience. But, like a lesser Mozart—and the Mozart of a particular mood—Pater proffers us his engaging *allegro*. The aim of all his art—its light but successful endeavour—is summed up in the title of one of the prettiest of his prints and pictures. It is, *Le désir de plaire*.

Presently we leave that world of graceful fantasy, which Watteau invented, and his pupils prolonged— a world in which dainty refreshments are served to chosen companies under serene skies—and, still in the full middle of the Eighteenth Century, we are face to face with the one great artist of that age whom Watteau never affected. Chardin was the painter of the *bourgeoisie*. With a persistence just as marked as that of the most homely Dutchmen, but with a refinement of feeling to which they were generally strangers and which gave distinction to his treatment of his theme, he devoted himself to the chronicle of prosaic virtues. In his Art, no trace of the selected garden, of the elegant gallantries, of the excitement of Love in the gay or luscious weather. The honest townspeople know hardly a break in their measured sobriety. They are mothers of families; the cares of the *ménage* press on them; house-work has to be got through; children taught, admonished, corrected. Never before or since have these scenes of the kitchen, the schoolroom, or the middle-class parlour, been painted with such dignity, such truth, such intimacy, and such permissible and fortunate reserve. We see them to perfection in Chardin's prints—in the prints, I mean, that were made after him, for he himself engraved never. There are two other sides of his Art which the contemporary line-engravings do not show. One of them is his mastery of still-life—his great and exceptional nobility in the treatment of it. There is just a hint of that, it is true, in the delicate engraving of *L'Œconome*, and the broader, richer engraving of *La Pourvoyeuse*; but for any real indication of it, and even that is but a partial one, we must come to Jules de Goncourt's etching of the *Gobelet d'Argent*, which suggests the luminousness, the characteristic *reflets*, and the *touche grasse* of the master. The other side of Chardin's talent which the engravings do not represent, is his later skill in professed portraiture, and especially in portraiture in pastel, to which the fashionable but well-merited triumphs of Latour directed him in his old age. But

the deliberate ·limitations of the Eighteenth Century
prints do not in any way invalidate the excellence, the
completeness even, of their performance. The collector
should address himself to their study. A little diligence, a little patience, and a hundred pounds, and it
would not be impossible to form a collection in which
nothing should be wanting. I remember that I gave
M. Lacroix or M. Rapilly, in Paris, not more than
seventy-five francs an impression for pieces in extraordinarily fine condition, and with margins almost intact.

Chardin went on working till he was eighty years
old. He enjoyed popularity, and he outlived it.
From 1738 to 1757, there were issued, in close succession, the engravings, about fifty in number, which,
with all their differences, and with all sorts of interesting notes about them, M. Emanuel Bocher has con-
scientiously and lovingly catalogued. They were
published at a couple of francs or so apiece; their
appearance was wont to be welcomed in little notices
in the *Mercure de France*, just as the *Standard* or the
Times to-day might applaud a new Whistler or a new
Frank Short; and they hung everywhere on *bourgeois*
walls. The canvases which they translated were owned,
some by a King of France, and some by a foreign
Sovereign. Little in the work of the whole century
had greater right to popularity than the *Jeu de l'Oye*,
with its exquisite and homely grace — Surugue has
perfectly engraved it — *L'Etude du Dessein*, austere and
masterly (Le Bas has rendered well the figure's attitude
of absorption), *Le Bénédicité*, with the unaffected piety,

179

the simple contentment of the narrow home, and *La Gouvernante*, with the young woman's friendly camaraderie and yet solicitude for the boy who is her charge.

At last Fashion shifted. Chardin was in the shade. Even Diderot got tired of him; though it was only the distaste of a contemporary for an excellence too constantly repeated—and the artist betook himself, with vanished popularity, to changed labours. But the vogue had lasted long enough for his method to be imitated. Jeaurat tried to look at common life through Chardin's glasses. But Jeaurat did not catch the sentiment of Chardin as successfully as Lancret and Pater had caught the sentiment of Watteau. And along with a little humour, of which the print of the *Citrons de Javotte* affords a trace, he had some coarseness of his own which assorted ill with Chardin's homely but unalloyed refinement. Chardin was profound; Jeaurat, comparatively shallow. You look not without interest at the productions of the one; you enter thoroughly into the world of the other. The creation of Chardin—which his engravers pass on to us—has a sense of peace, of permanence, a curious reality.

Reality is that which to us of the present day seems above all things lacking to the laboured and obvious moralities of Greuze, who was voluptuous when he posed to be innocent, and was least convincing when he sought to be moral. Yet Greuze, when he was not the painter of the too seductive damsel, but of family piety and family afflictions, must have spoken to his

own time with seeming sincerity. Even a liberal
philosophy—the philosophy of Diderot—patted him
gently on the back, and invited him to reiterate his
commendable and salutary lessons. But the philosophy
was a little sentimental, or it would scarcely have continued to Greuze the encouragement it had withdrawn
from Chardin. The Greuze pictures chiefly engraved
in his own time were his obtrusive moralities. They
now find little favour. But Levasseur's print of *La
Laitière* and Massard's of *La Cruche cassée*—elaborate,
highly wrought, and suggesting that ivory flesh texture
which the master obtained when he was most dexterously luxurious—these will fascinate the Sybarite,
legitimately, during still many generations.

Before the first successes of the painter of that
Laitière and that *Cruche cassée*, there was flourishing
at Court, under the Pompadour's patronage, the "rose-
water Raphael," the "bastard of Rubens." This was
François Boucher. The region of his art lay as far
indeed from reality as did Watteau's "enchanted isle,"
and it had none of the rightful magnetism of that
country of poetic dream. It was not, like Watteau's
land, that of a privileged and fortunate humanity,
but of

"False Gods, and Muses misbegot."

Where Boucher tried to be refined, he was insincere;
and where he was veracious, he was but picturesquely
gross. His notion of Olympus was that of a mountain
on which ample human forms might be undraped with

181

impunity. That Olympus of a limited imagination he frequented with industry. But, as a decorative painter, there is no need to undervalue his fertility and skill, his apparently inexhaustible though trivial impulse; and if few of his larger compositions have deserved those honours which they have obtained, of translation into elaborate line-engraving, hosts of the chalk studies which are so characteristic of his facile talent were appropriately reproduced in fac-simile by the ingenious inventions of Demarteau. These fac-similes were very cheap indeed not many years ago, nor are they to-day expensive. Of Boucher's more considered work, engraved in line, *La Naissance de Vénus*, by Duflos, and *Jupiter et Léda*, by Ryland, are important and agreeable, and, as times go, by no means costly instances.

Fragonard, besides being a nobler colourist than Boucher—as the silvery pinks and creamy whites of the *Chemise en levée*, at the Louvre, would alone be enough to indicate — was at once a master of more chastened taste and of less impotent passion. He was of the succession of the Venetians. Fragonard came to Paris from the South—from amidst the olives and the flowers of Grasse—and he retained to the end a measure of the warmth and sunshine of Provence. The artistic eagerness, the hurried excitement, of some of his work, is much in accord with his often fiery themes; but in *L'Heureuse Fécondité*, *Les Beignets*, and *La Bonne Mère* (all of them engraved by De Launay) the collector can possess himself of compositions in which Fragonard depicted domestic life in his own lively way.

182

That is only one side of his mind, and, like his love of dignified and ordered artificial Landscape, it is little known. Elsewhere he showed himself a skilled and an appreciative observer of wholly secular character, and he embodied upon many a canvas his conception of Love—it was not to him the constant devotion of a life, but the unhesitating tribute of an hour. *Le Verre d'Eau* and *Le Pot au Lait* are good gay prints, but not for every one. In *Le Chiffre d'Amour*, Affection, which with Fragonard is rarely inelegant, becomes for a moment sentimental.

Contemporary with Fragonard were a group of artists who, more than Fragonard, left Allegory aside, and exercised their imagination only in a rearrangement of the real. These were the French Little Masters: amongst them, Lavreince, the Saint-Aubins, Baudouin, Eisen, Moreau le jeune. They had seen the life of Paris — Baudouin, the debased side of it; but even Baudouin had some feeling for elegance and comedy. Eisen was above all an illustrator. Augustin de Saint-Aubin, a man of various talents, displayed in little things, is studied most agreeably in those two pretty and well-disposed interiors, *Le Concert* and *Le Bal paré*. They are his most prized pieces; and prettiness having often more money value than greatness, they are worth more than any Watteaus— they are worth full twenty pounds the pair. And that is all I can afford to say of Augustin de Saint-Aubin. Lavreince and Moreau must be spoken of a little more fully.

Nicholas Lavreince was by birth a Swede, but,
educated in Paris and practising his art there, he was
more French than the French. Edmond and Jules de
Goncourt, the best historians of the Painting of the
time, do not much appreciate him : at least in comparison with Baudouin. They say that Baudouin's method
was larger and more artistic than Lavreince's, whose
way was generally the way of somewhat painful finish.
I have seen by Lavreince one agreeable water-colour
which has all the impulse of the first intention, and, so
far, belies the De Goncourts' judgment. But the judgment is doubtless true in the main. That does not
make Lavreince a jot less desirable for the collectors of
prints. Both he and Baudouin wrought to be engraved,
but Lavreince's work was done with a much larger
measure of reference to that subsequent interpretation.
The true *gouaches* of Lavreince are of extraordinary
rarity ; and if their method is in some respects less
excellent than that of the companion-works of Baudouin, their themes are more presentable. Lavreince,
in his brilliant portrayal of a luxurious, free-living
Society, sometimes allowed himself a liberty our century might resent ; but Baudouin's license—save in such
an exquisite subject as that of *La Toilette*, which depicts the slimmest and most graceful of his models—
was on a par with that of Rétif de la Bretonne. A
proof before all letters of the delightful *Toilette*—
engraved so delicately by Ponce—is worth, when it
appears, ten or twelve pounds : a more ordinary, a less
rare impression, is worth perhaps three or four.

Baudouin—in too much of his work—was the portrayer of coarse intrigue in humble life and high: Lavreince and Moreau, masters of polite Genre, with subjects wider and more varied, the chroniclers of conversations not inevitably *tête-à-tête*. For vividness and intellectual delicacy of expression in the individual heads, one must give the palm to Moreau. The De Goncourts claim for him also pre-eminence in composition; but in one piece at least—in the *Assemblée au Concert*, engraved by Dequevauviller—Lavreince runs Moreau hard. And Lavreince, I can't help thinking, has an invention scarcely less refined. What can be gentler, yet what if gentle can be more abundant comedy than his, in the *Directeur des Toilettes?* —the scene in which a prosperous Abbé, an arbiter of Taste in women's dress, dictates the choice to his delightful friend, or busily preserves her from the chances of error. And very noteworthy is Lavreince's way of availing himself of all the opportunities for beautiful design—beautiful line, at all events—which were afforded him by the noble interiors in which there passed the action of his drama. Those interiors are of the days of Louis Seize, and are a little more severe, a little less intricate, than the interiors of Louis Quinze. Musical instruments, often beautiful of form—harp, harpsichord, and violoncello—play their part in these pictorial compositions. Prints from Lavreince, like prints from Moreau, are too gay and too agreeable not to be always valued. England and America will surely take to them, as France has done long ago.

It has been claimed for Moreau—Moreau " le jeune,"
to distinguish him from his less eminent brother—that
he is yet more exact than Lavreince is, in his record
of the fashions of his period in furniture and dress.
And sometimes, on this very account, his effect is more
prosaic—just as at the contemporary theatre the accessories are apt to dominate or dwarf the persons of the
drama. Yet Moreau's people have generally some interest of individuality and liveliness, and these characteristics are nowhere better seen than in the two series
which he designed to show the life of a great lady from
the moment of motherhood and the daily existence of
a man of fashion. These prints—such as *C'est un Fils,
Monsieur ; La Sortie de l'Opera ; La Grande Toilette*—
should be possessed, let me tell the collector, with the
" A. P. D. Q." still upon them : not in a later state.
Moreau, besides being a charming and observant
draughtsman, was himself a delicate engraver ; but he
left to others (Romanet, Baquoy, and Malbeste amongst
them) the business of reproducing his story of the ruling
classes—of the leaders of Society—and it was sufficiently popularised. Having regard to what it was—
a story, to some people, of irritating even though of
elegant triviality—perhaps it was as well for those
ruling classes of the *ancien régime* that it did not go
further—that it was not actually broadcast. Of Beau-
marchais's pungent comedy the saying has since passed
round, that it was the Revolution "*en action.*" So
envy or contempt might surely have been fostered
by the wide-spread perusal of Moreau's exquisite,

unvarnished record, and the Revolution have been advanced by a day.

With Moreau's art, the Eighteenth Century closes. There is an end of its luxury and its amenity—an end of the lover who insists and the lady who but lightly forbids. There followed after it the boneless, nerveless, still eminently graceful pseudo-classicism of Prud'hon, and the sterner pseudo-classicism of David, which recalled the ideal of men to a more strenuous life. But that life was not of the Eighteenth Century. The inflexible David, like the dreamy Prud'hon, was an artist for another age. The graceful, graceless Eighteenth Century—with its own faults, and no less with its own virtues—had said its last word. Familiar and luxurious, tolerant and engaging, it had expressed through Art the last of its so easily supported sorrows and its so easily forgotten loves.

CHAPTER X

*The range of Turner Prints—His earlier Engravers
—His " Liber Studiorum "—Its etchings, proofs,
completed mezzotints—Its money value—" Liber "
Collectors — The " Southern Coast " Series — The
" England and Wales "—The " Richmondshire " Prints
—" Ports " and " Rivers of England "—The Turner
Prints secure the Master's fame.*

TURNER prints constitute a class apart. The prints
which others made after Turner's drawings and pictures,
the prints he executed to some extent or wholly himself,
the engravings in line and the engravings in mezzotint,
are all of them wont to be collected not so much as
part of the representation of a particular method of
work, but rather as the representation of an individual
genius and of a whole school of the most highly
skilled craftsmen.

The Turner prints range in period from a year at
least as early as 1794 to a year at least as late as 1856—
for though Turner was then dead, one or two of the finest
engravers whom he had employed were at that date still
labouring in the popularisation of his pieces. They
range in size from the dainty vignette a couple of inches
high, to the extensive plate — a wonder of executive
skill, yet often, too, a wonder of misplaced ingenuity—

188

which may be three feet long. Between them come
the very masterpieces of the landscape engraving of our
century—line-engravings like the "Southern Coast";
mezzotint supported by etching, like the "Liber Studiorum." They range in value between a couple of
shillings or so—the price, when you can get the print,
of a specimen of the early publications in the "Copper-
plate Magazine"—to, say, well shall we say to £50?
—the price of an exceptional proof of a fine, rare
subject in "Liber." In point of number, those of
which account may reasonably be taken by the student
of our greatest Landscape artist through the charming
medium of his prints—or if you will by the student of
Engraving who finds in pieces after Turner alone a
sufficient range of method in the illustration of Landscape—in point of number those which there need be
no desire to ignore or forget, reach, roundly speaking,
to four or five hundred. It is possible to make the
study and acquisition of them the main business of
the life of an intelligent collector.

Mr. W. G. Rawlinson is perhaps amongst existing
connoisseurs the one whose knowledge of the engravings
by Turner, and after him, is the widest and most exact.
Mr. Rawlinson has greatly extended the sum of his
own knowledge since he penned that catalogue raisonné of the "Liber Studiorum" which remains his
only published contribution to the history of the
prints of Turner. The book is of much value; but
though, broadly considered, it remains an adequate
and serviceable guide, there must by this time be a

good many corrections in the matter of "States"—
rarely is it that the issue of a First Edition of a descriptive catalogue of engraved work does not elicit,
from one source or another, some information, the
existence of which the author had had no reason to
surmise. And, moreover, it may be hoped that Mr.
Rawlinson's more extended studies in the field of his
particular inquiry will bear fruit some day in the
production of another volume, devoted this time to
the tale of the great series of Line-Engravings and
the less numerous productions in pure Mezzotint.
"Liber," remember—the master-work, which is thus
far the only one to have been elaborately discussed or
chronicled by any critic—is the result of a combination
of Mezzotint with Etching. But we will go back a
little, and will take the prints—or such of them as
there is cause to mention—in due order.

I recollect Mr. Rawlinson saying to me, not many
months ago—in speaking of the little publications of
the "Copper-plate Magazine" and of such-like small
and early work—that Turner was never properly engraved till he was engraved by James Basire; and I
think, upon the whole, that this is true. At a later
period, Turner himself protested that he was never
properly, at all events never quite perfectly, engraved,
till he was engraved by John Pye—but then that
was for a quite different order of work from that which
occupied him in the first years of his skilled and accomplished practice. What Mr. Rawlinson meant was,
that whereas the engraver—tasteful and in a measure

190

delicate, yet slight and wanting wholly in subtlety of realisation and treatment—who did the little prints in the "Copper-plate Magazine," such as the *Carlisle* and the *Wakefield*, failed to translate into his art all the really translatable qualities of the immature yet interesting work to which he addressed himself, Basire, in the brilliant and solid prints which served as head-pieces to the "Oxford Almanacks," from 1799 to 1811, did the most thorough justice to their mainly architectural themes. It was in the year in which Basire finished—and Turner's art, by this time, had, of course, greatly changed—that there was executed by John Pye the very work (*Pope's Villa*) which extorted from Turner what it may be was his first warm tribute of admiration to anybody who translated him. But four years before this, Turner, with Charles Turner, the engraver in mezzotint, had begun the publication of the immortal series of " Liber Studiorum."

The set of prints which Turner issued as his " Liber Studiorum "—with an allusion, tolerably evident, to the " Liber Veritatis " of Claude — is but one series of several with which the English master of Landscape occupied himself during the fifty years, or more, of his working life. But it is the first series that was conceived by him; and it is, in the best sense, the most ambitious; and it remains the noblest and the most representative. In its actual execution Turner had a greater hand — an incomparably greater hand — than in that of any of its successors; and its scheme permitted a variety, an effective suddenness of transition, denied to the artist when, in later years, he was depicting that portion of the county of Yorks which is known as Richmondshire, or the "Southern Coast," or the "Rivers of France," or the "Ports of England," or even all the places which it pleased him to choose for one of the most elaborate of his publications, "The Picturesque Views in England and Wales." A long tether was allowed him, unquestionably, in some of these sets; but in the "Liber"—as it is called, briefly and affectionately, by collector and student—there was no question of tether at all. In it, a subject from Classical Mythology might stand side by side with a subject drawn from English barton and hedgerow—I am, as it were, naming *Procris and Cephalus, Æsacus and Hesperie,* the exquisite though homely *Straw Yard,* the entirely prosaic *Farm Yard with a Cock.* The interior of a London church, with its Georgian altar and its pews cosily curtained for the most respectable of *bourgeois,* might be presented in near neighbourhood to some study which Turner had recorded of the eternal hills, or of a great storm that gathered, rolled over, and passed away from Solway Moss.

I have used the word "study," since it is Turner's own. But each plate in "Liber Studiorum" is much more than a study. It is a finished composition. Turner spared neither time nor pains—though in this case, as in others, he was careful, where that was possible, to spare money—in making his work all that the wisest lover of his genius might expect it to be. Whatever rivalry there was with the "Liber Veritatis" of Claude,—

—the later portions of which were issuing from the house of Boydell at the very moment that Turner was planning the " Liber "—the rivalry was conducted upon no equal terms. I say nothing in depreciation of Claude's " Liber Veritatis." In it, one of the greatest practitioners of mezzotint engraving—Richard Earlom ,—reproduced, with learned simplicity, Claude's masterly memoranda—the sometimes slender yet always stately drawings in the preparation of which Nature had counted for something, and Art had counted for more. Claude's bistre sketches, by their dignity and style — even the hurried visitor to Chatsworth may know that—are akin to the landscapes of Rembrandt, to the studies of Titian. But the artist of the " Liber Veritatis" worked in haste, worked purposely in slightness, and more than one generation separated him from the engraver who was to execute the plates. Turner worked with elaboration, and worked at leisure, and he etched upon the plates, himself, the leading lines of his composition, and he was in contact with the engravers, and his directions to these accomplished craftsmen were rightly fastidious and endlessly minute.

Claude too was an etcher, yet it is not in the " Liber Veritatis " — it is in the rare and early States of his *Shepherd and Shepherdess Conversing,* of his *Cowherd* (" Le Bouvier "), of his *Cattle in Stormy Weather*— that (as a previous chapter has insisted) we are to find proof of his skilled familiarity with that means of expression which Turner employed as the basis of his work in the " Liber." Claude, when he etched, etched

for Etching's sake, and used with pleasure and with
ease the resources of the etcher's art. Turner restricted
Etching within narrower limits. When one remembers
the circumstance that, having etched the outlines on
the plate, he took a dozen or a score, perhaps, of
impressions from it before he caused the work in
mezzotint to be added, it is difficult to assert that he
did not attach a certain value to the etched outlines.
And indeed they are of extraordinary significance and
strength : they show economy of labour, certainty of
vision and of hand. It is very well that they, as well
as the finished plates, should be collected. But, in his
pleasure in possessing himself of these rare, noble
things, the collector must not allow himself to forget
that they were essentially a preparation and a susten-
ance for that which was to follow—for that admirable
mezzotint on which the subtlest lights and shadows of
the picture, its infinite and indescribably delicate gradations, were intended to depend.

Of this Mezzotint it is time to speak. Its employment, though it proved—as I think I have implied
already—wonderfully conducive to the quality of the
" Liber " plates, was not resolved upon at first. The
process of aquatint, in which much work was done
about that time—in which, only a very few years
before " Liber " began, Turner's friend, Thomas Girtin,
had produced some broadly-treated views of Paris—
had, at first, been thought of. Negotiations were
opened with Lewis, and he executed in aquatint one
of the plates, which Turner did indeed eventually use,

but which he was careful not to use in the earliest numbers of the publication. The superiority of Mezzotint he recognised quite clearly. He employed the best mezzotinters. He busied himself to instruct them as to the effects that he desired. He learnt the art himself, and himself mezzotinted, with great exquisiteness, ten out of the seventy-one plates. He worked, in later stages, upon all the rest of them; obtaining generally the most refined beauty, but working in such a fashion as to exhaust the plate with extravagant swiftness. Then he touched and retouched, almost as Mr. Whistler has touched and retouched the plates of his Venetian etchings. So delicate, so evanescent, rarity is not an aim, but a need, with them.

The publication of the "Liber"—the great undertaking of the early middle period of Turner's art—began in 1807, and its issue was arrested in the year 1819. It was never completed—seventy-one finished plates were given to the world out of the hundred that were meant to be. But Turner had by that time proceeded far with the remainder, of which twenty plates, more or less finished, testified to a gathering rather than a lessening strength. By the non-publication of these later plates, the collector—if not necessarily the student—is deprived of several of the noblest illustrations of Turner's genius. Nothing in the whole series shows an elegance more dignified than that which the *Stork and Aqueduct* displays; the mystery of dawn is magnificent in the *Stonehenge*; and never was pastoral landscape—the England of field and wood and sloping hillside—more engaging or suggestive than in the *Crowhurst*.

The mention of these plates—the hint it gives us as to difference of subject and of aim—brings up the question of the various classes of composition into which Turner thought proper to divide his work. His advertisement of the publication affords a proof of how widely representative the work was intended to be; nor, indeed, did the execution at all fall short of Turner's hope in this respect. The work was to be—and we know, now, how fully it became—an illustration of Landscape Composition, classed as follows: "Historical, Mountainous, Pastoral, Marine, and Architectural." And further, it is said in the advertisement, "Each number contains five engravings in mezzotint: one subject of each class." But Turner, in these matters, was extraordinarily unmethodical—I should like to say "muddled." Each number did contain five engravings, and they were "in mezzotint," with the preparation in etching; but it was by no means always that there was one subject of each class, for Turner divided the Pastoral into simple and what he described as "elegant" or "epic" Pastoral (Mr. Roget thinks that the "E.P." means "epic"), and the very first number contained a Historical, a Marine, an Architectural subject, but it contained no Mountainous, for the Pastoral was represented in both of its forms ("P." and "E.P.").

The actual publication was exceedingly irregular. Sometimes two numbers—or two parts, as we may better call them—were issued at once. Sometimes there would be an interval of several years between the issue of a couple of parts. There is no doubt that as the work progressed Turner felt increasingly the neglect under which it suffered. Gradually he lost interest in its actual issue—but, never for a moment in its excellence.

Charles Turner, the admirable mezzotint engraver—who, it should hardly be necessary to say, was no relation of the greater man—had charge of "Liber" in its early stages. The prints of the first parts bore an inscription to the effect that they were "Published by C. Turner, 50 Warren Street, Fitzroy Square." But in 1811—when three years had elapsed since the publication of the fourth part—the fifth came out as "Published by Mr. Turner, Queen Anne Street, West"—and "Mr. Turner" meant, of course, the author of the work. Charles Turner, who had engraved in mezzotint every plate contained in the four parts with whose publication he was concerned, engraved, likewise, several of the succeeding pieces. Thus his share in the production of "Liber" was greater than that of any of his brethren. William Say's came next to his in importance—importance measured by amount of labour—and Mr. Rawlinson has pointed out that William Say approached his work with little previous preparation by the rendering of Landscape. The remark is, in some degree, applicable to most of Say's associates. The engraver in mezzotint, at that time, as in earlier times, flourished chiefly by reproducing Portraiture. Raphael Smith and William Ward—great artists who

197

were still living when the "Liber" was executed, but who had no part in the performance—had been employed triumphantly, a very little earlier, in popularising that delightful art of Morland, in which landscape had so large a place. Dunkarton, Thomas Lupton, Clint, Easling, Annis, Dawe, S. W. Reynolds, and Hodges complete the list of the engravers in mezzotint who worked upon the "Liber." Admirable artists many of them were, but the collector, if he is a student, cannot forget how much the master, the originator, dominated over all.

Mr. Ruskin and several subsequent writers have written, with varying degrees of eloquence, of originality, and, I may add, of common sense, as to the moral, emotional, or intellectual message the "Liber" may be taken to convey. This is scarcely the place in which to seek to decipher with exhaustive thoroughness a communication that is on the whole complicated and on the whole mysterious. The reader may be referred to the last pages of the final volume of "Modern Painters" for what is at all events the most impressive statement that a prose-poet can deliver as to the gloomy significance of Turner's work. Mr. Stopford Brooke—rich in sensibility and in imaginative perceptiveness—follows a good deal in Mr. Ruskin's track. I doubt if Mr. Hamerton or Mr. Cosmo Monkhouse — instructive critics of a cooler school— endorse the verdict of unmitigated gloom, and I have myself (in a chapter in a now well-nigh forgotten essay of my youth) ventured to hold forth upon the

intervals of peace and rest which " Liber Studiorum " shows in its scenes of solitude and withdrawal: the morning light, clear and serene, in the meadows below Oakhampton Castle; the graver silence of sunset as one looks wistfully from heights above the Wye, to where, under the endless skies, the stream deploys to the river. I am referring, of course, to the *Oakhampton Castle* subject, and to the *Severn and Wye;* but the argument might have been sustained by allusion to many another print.

More important to our present purpose than to settle accurately its moral mission or to agree upon the sentiment of this or that particular plate, is it to value properly the sterling and artistic virtues which " Liber " makes manifest. Of these, however, there is one thing only that I care to emphasise here. Let all beauties of detail be discovered; but let us even here, and in lines that are of necessity brief, lay stress upon the all-important part played in the plates of " Liber " by one old-fashioned virtue, that will yet be fresh again when some of those that may seem to supplant it have indeed waxed old. It is the virtue of Composition. " Liber Studiorum " shows, in passage after passage of its draughtsmanship, close reference to Nature, deep knowledge of her secrets; but it shows I think yet more the unavoidable conviction, alike of true worker and true connoisseur, that Nature is, for the artist, not a Deity but a material: not a tyrant but a servant. In the near and faithful study of Nature—and nowhere more completely than in the prints of " Liber "—Turner did much that had been left undone by predecessors. But he was not opposed to them—he was allied to them—in his recognition of the fact that his art must do much more than merely reproduce. " Nature," said Goethe, " Nature has excellent intentions." And by Composition, by choice, by economy of means, sometimes by very luxury of hidden labour, it is the business of the artist to convey these intentions to the beholders of his work. How much does he receive? How much of himself, of his creative mind, must we exact that he shall bestow ?

Let us come down, immediately, to money matters, and other practical things for the collector's benefit.

It is still possible, here and there, in an auction room, to buy an original set of " Liber Studiorum "—a set, that is, as Turner issued it—but it is never desirable. For Turner, who was not only a great poet with brush and pencil, and scraper and etching needle, but an exceedingly keen hard bargainer and man of business, took horrible care (or just care, if we choose to call it so) that the original subscribers to his greatest serial should never get sets consisting altogether of the fine impressions. He mixed the good with the second-rate : the second-rate with the bad. It was not till collectors took to studying the pieces for themselves, and making up collections by purchase of odd pieces here and there —rejecting much, accepting something—that any sets were uniformly good. The first fine set, perhaps, was that, in various States, which was amassed by Mr. Stokes, and passed on to his niece, Miss Mary Constance

Clarke. To have the marks of these ownerships at the back of a print, is—in ninety-nine cases out of a hundred—to have evidence of excellence. Twenty years ago, one could buy such a print, now and then, at Halsted's, the ancient dealer's, in Rathbone Place; and have an instructive chat to boot, with an old-world personage who had had speech with "Mr. Turner." Even now, in an auction room, one may get such a print sometimes. Another of the very early collectors was Sir John Hippesley, who bought originally on Halsted's recommendation, and who — having been for years devoted to works of other masters— ended by breakfasting, so to speak, on "Liber Studiorum:" on the chair opposite to him, as he sat at his meal, a fine print was wont to be placed. Amongst living connoisseurs, Mr. Henry Vaughan and Mr. J. E. Taylor, Mr. Stopford Brooke and Mr. W. G. Rawlinson, have notable collections of very varying size and importance. Mr. Rawlinson believes much more than I do— if I understand him aright — in the desirability of possessing engravers' trial proofs — in a certain late stage. Most engravers' proofs are, of course, mere preparations, curious and interesting, but in themselves far less desirable than the finished plates to whose effects of deliberate and attained beauty they can but vaguely approximate. Of course if you are so exceedingly lucky a man as to have been able to pounce upon the particular proof which was the last of the series, you possess a fine and incontestable thing; but generally an early impression of the First published

State represents the subject more safely and assuredly ; and, failing that, an early impression of the Second State ; and so on. An indication of priority is no doubt well — but it is well chiefly for the feebler brethren. You must train your eye. Having trained it, you must learn to rely on it. Books and the knowledge of States are useful, but are not sufficient.

In the few years that elapsed between the establishment of "Liber" as avowedly fit material for the diligence and outlay of the collector, and the great sale of the "remainders" in Turner's own collection—which only left Queen Anne Street in 1873, some two-and-twenty years after his death—prices for fine impressions of the "Liber" plates, bought separately, were high. Then, in 1873, during that long sale at Christie's, a flood of prints, and many of them very fine ones, came upon the market. "Would they ever be absorbed ? " it was asked. They were absorbed very quickly. But just until they were absorbed, it was, naturally, possible, not only to choose (at the dealer's, chiefly, who bought big lots ; at the Colnaghi's and Mrs. Noseda's, particularly)—it was possible to choose sagaciously, out of so great a number, and to choose cheaply too. Then "markets hardened." The various writings calling attention to the wisdom of collecting had probably their effect. Then things slackened again. And now, though rare proofs and very fine impressions—which are what should be most cared about—hold their own, there is a certain lull in the activity of buying. The undesirable impression goes for very little. Yet the fluctuations, such as they are, either way, are of no vast importance. Of any but the very rarest, or very finest subjects, six to twelve guineas gets a good First State. Three to six guineas may be the price of a good Second. A Third or Fourth or Fifth State fetches less, unless—as in an exceptional instance, like the *Calm*—it is preferable. Of all the different subjects, the rarest is *Ben Arthur*. In a fine impression —with the cloudland and the shadows not impenetrably massive—it is exceedingly impressive. But never as a thing of power should I rate it above *Solway Moss* or *Hind Head Hill*; or, as a thing of beauty, above *Severn and Wye*.

No great collection of the "Liber Studiorum" has been sold of late years, but if we go back to the year 1887, we can give a few prices culled from the catalogue of the Buccleugh Sale. An engraver's proof of the *Woman with a Tambourine* fetched £15, 15s. there ; an engraver's proof of *Basle*, £27 ; a proof of the *Mount St. Gothard*, which at least must have had the virtue of approaching finish, fell to Colnaghi's bid of £55 ; the First State of the *Holy Island Cathedral*, which sold for £3, 3s., must either have been poor or monstrously cheap, though the plate is one in which, even to the collector with the most trained eye, the possession of the First State is not strictly necessitated : the subject is among those—and they are not so very few—in which the Second State, well chosen, is altogether adequate. The First State of the *Hind Head Hill* reached £14, 14s. ; the First of the *London from*

Greenwich, with its noble panorama of the long stretched Town and winding river, reached £15, 15s. A proof of the *Windmill and Lock* reached £31; a First State of the *Severn and Wye*, £21; a First State of the *Procris and Cephalus*, £11; a First State of the *Watercress Gatherers*, £11, 11s. The pure etchings, which I have written of in an earlier paragraph in this chapter, sell, generally speaking, for three or four guineas apiece; the etching of the *Isis*, which is extremely rare, fetched at the Bucclcugh auction £13, 13s. By the Fine Art Society £74 was paid for a First State of the *Ben Arthur*. The plates least eagerly sought, or in inferior condition, went for all sorts of prices between a pound or two and four or five guineas. I think, as far as value may be judged without the presence of the particular impressions which were sold, the little list I have now given above may fairly indicate it, but no quite thorough indication can be got without an immense accumulation of detail, and, on the reader's part, an immense knowledge in interpreting it. It is not unintentionally that we have lingered long over the "Liber." But more than one other great series must engage at all events a brief attention.

In 1814 began the amous "Southern Coast" series, which was brought to an end in 1827. For these prints, engraved in admirable and masculine "line," chiefly by the brothers George and William Cooke, Turner had made water colours, whilst as a preparation for the "Liber," he had made but slight though finely considered sepia drawings—mere guides and hints to himself and the engravers he employed upon the plates: things whose significance was to be enlarged: not things to be merely copied and scrupulously kept to. In quite tolerable condition the ordinary impressions of the "Southern Coast" plates are to be had in large book-form; but the collector, buying single piece by single piece, at one or two or three guineas each, seeks generally impressions before letters or with the scratched title. Of course the variations in condition are noticeable, but in the firm "line" of the "Southern Coast," they are at least much less noticeable than in the delicate and evanescent mezzotints of "Liber."

The year in which the publication of the "Southern Coast" was finished — when prints picturesque and vivid, and in some cases, as in the *Clovelly* of William Miller, perfectly exquisite, had been presented of the most interesting seaboard places between Minehead and Whitstable—that year was the period at which the publication of the third great series, the "England and Wales," was begun. It was to have extended to thirty parts or more: each part containing four subjects. But, like "Liber," it received, on its first issue, no full and satisfying measure of encouragement, and though it reached its twenty-fourth part, it did not go further. It was published at about two guineas and a half a part. "England and Wales" sets forth with great elaboration of line engraving the characteristics of the later middle period of Turner's art, so far as black and white can set it forth at all. That was the period in which subject was most complicated and most ample—even unduly ample—and in which Turner dealt at once with the most intricate line and with all sorts of problems of colour, atmosphere, illumination. The work of all that period, from 1827, say, to ten years onwards —with many of its merits, its inevitable shortcomings, and its immense ambition—the "England and Wales" represents. The work of various engravers trained by Turner for the interpretation of all that was most complicated, it will ever be interesting and valuable. Such prints as *Stamford*, *Llanthony Abbey*, and the noble *Yarmouth* stand ever in the front line. The last, like the *Clovelly* of the "Southern Coast," is a work of William Miller, the old Quaker engraver, whose rendering of Turner's delicate skies no other line engraver has approached—not even William Cooke, who did so well that troop of light little wind clouds in the *Margate* of the "Southern Coast." Admirable then, indeed, many of these things must be allowed to be; and in this sense they are almost unique, that scarcely anything else has possessed their qualities. Yet on the whole one admires "England and Wales" with reservations. One's heart goes out more thoroughly to "Liber" and to "Southern Coast."

There are other series which must not be passed over altogether — the "Richmondshire Set," of which the first print was executed, I think, in 1820, though the whole volume was not issued till 1823. It too is in line: the finest print of all, perhaps the *Ingleborough*. Then there are six "Ports of England:" impressive,

varied little mezzotints, unsupported by etching—prints
in one of which Turner has set down, for all time, his
clear, unequalled perception of the beauty of the Scarborough coast-line. Then there are the "Rivers of
England," with the noble *Arundel*, the restful *Totness*.
Then there are, in line, the almost over-dainty yet
miraculous little prints of "Rivers of France." Then
there are the wonderful vignettes in illustration of
Walter Scott. These, like the illustrations to the
Rogers' "Poems" and the "Italy," with which they
have the most affinity, are luminous and gem-like.
The Rogers illustrations of course deteriorate in later
editions; the "Italy" of 1830 and the "Poems" of
1834 are the ones that should be possessed; and were
the present volume of a wider scope and addressed to
the book-collector, I should allow myself to say here
what it seems I do say here, without "allowing myself"—that the collector should get, if possible, a
copy in the original boards, and may give £5 for
that as safely as a couple of sovereigns for a re-bound
copy.

Turner is represented on many a side by the engraver's
art, and in most cases with singular good fortune. For
some, there are the vignettes which have the finish of
Cellini work. For some, it may be, the large, more
recent plates, the *Modern Italy* and *Ancient Italy*, that
hang, I cannot help considering, rather ineffectively
upon the wall: too big, not for their place, but for
their method of execution — and yet, like so many,
wonderful. He is represented best of all perhaps in

works of middle scale — in the virile line of the
" Southern Coast," and the unapproachable mezzotint
and etching of the " Liber." If everything that he has
wrought with brush or pencil were extinguished, these
things, living, would make immortal his fame.

CHAPTER XI

The healthy appreciation of Mezzotint—Its faculty of conveying the painter's very touch—Landscape Scenes in Mezzotint — Comparative Rarity of Landscapes — The Constables — Vast volume of Rare Pieces and Portraits — The Prints after Sir Joshua Reynolds— Dr. Hamilton's Catalogue — The smaller number of Gainsboroughs — Increased appreciation of Romney —Mr. Percy Horne's book on these men — George Morland—The cost of Mezzotints now, and when first issued.

OF modern fashions in Print Collecting, the appreciation of Mezzotints is assuredly one of the healthiest, and—apart from the question of the very high prices to which mezzotints have lately been forced—there is only one drawback to the pleasure of the Collector in bringing them together : the collector of mezzotints has to resign himself to do without original work. The scraping of the plate in these broad masses of shadow and light—a method immensely popular as means of interpretation or translation of the painter's touch—has from the days of the invention of the process by Ludwig von Siegen to the days of its latest practice, never greatly commended itself to the original artist as a method for fresh design. There are a few exquisite exceptions ; and perhaps there is no sufficient reason why there should not be more; but the exceptions best known, and most likely to be cited, the prints of Turner's "Liber Studiorum," are exceptions only in so far as regards that small proportion of the whole—about ten amongst the published plates — wrought by Turner himself.

And, further, the collector, if he cares much for Landscape subjects, will note that landscapes in mezzotint are comparatively few. It was in the Eighteenth Century that the production of mezzotint was most voluminous; and the Eighteenth Century took little interest in Landscape. In the earlier half of our own century—ere yet the art had almost ceased to be practised—the world was given a few famous sets of landscapes in mezzotint; but they were very few. Turner's "Liber" (with its backbone of etching) was followed by the half-dozen pieces of the "Ports of England," and by "Rivers of England," or "River Scenery," as it is sometimes called, "after Turner and Girtin;" and then, well in the middle of the half-century, we were endowed with the delightful, now highly prized mezzotints, which were executed by David Lucas after the works of Constable, homely when they were sombre, homely too when they were most sparkling and alive. They too—like the "Liber" prints of Turner—profited by the supervision of the creative artist. The tendency of Mr. Lucas was to make them too black, and perhaps a little too massive. Sparkle and vivacity were wanted in any adequate renderings of Constable; and these, by Constable's own solicitude, and doubtless too by the adaptability of Lucas's talent, were eventually obtained. In our own day, several most meritorious artists—Wehrschmidt and Gerald Robinson and others—have done, in several branches, accomplished and interesting work in mezzotint, and Frank Short, in one print especially that I have in my mind after a Turner drawing—an Alpine subject—and again in a bold decisive mezzotint, *A Road in Yorkshire*, after Dewint (a road skirting the moors)—is altogether admirable. And, to name yet a third instance of the art of this so flexible and extraordinarily sympathetic translator, there is the quite wonderful little vision of the silvery grey Downs, after a sketch by Constable in the possession of Mr. Henry Vaughan, whose greater Constable, the *Hay Wain*, was generously made over to the nation, many years ago. The work of David Lucas, done under Constable's eye, never—not even in the radiant *Summerland* or in the steel-grey keenness of the *Spring*—for one moment excelled in delicacy of manipulation Frank Short's delightful rendering of that vision of the Downs. But I am not to dwell longer upon particular instances. We are brought back to a repetition of the fact that it is not, generally speaking, in examples of Landscape Art that the collector of mezzotints must find himself richest. The mezzotint collector's groups of landscapes will be limited. In the collection of religious compositions, of *genre* pieces, of theatrical subjects, of "fancy" subjects—in which that which is most "fancied" is the prettiness of the female sex—in sporting and in racing

211

subjects (amongst the latter there are a few most
admirable prints after George Stubbs), and most of
all, of course, in portraits, from the days of Lely to
the days of Lawrence, there will be opportunities of
filling portfolio after portfolio, drawer after drawer.

It is difficult, I think, for the collector—still more
for the student who has not a collector's practical interest in the matter—to realise what is actually the
extent of that contribution to the world's possessions
in the way of Art, which has been made, and all within
about two hundred years, by the engravers in mezzotint. Some eighteen years ago, an Irish amateur, Mr.
Challoner Smith, began the publication of a Catalogue
which when it was concluded, several years later, had
extended to five volumes. It was a colossal labour.
Styled by its compiler, "British Mezzotint Portraits,"
it really includes the chronicle of many things which
at least are not professedly portraits—yet it excludes
many too. Whatever it excludes, its bulk is such, that,
amongst the mass of its matter, it comprises full de-
scriptions of between four and five hundred plates by
one artist alone. The man is Faber, junior. Fifty
plates are chronicled by an engraver more modern of
character, more popular to-day — Richard Earlom;
amongst them, more than one of the *genre* or in-
cident pictures after Wright of Derby (in which a
difficult effect of chiaroscuro—an effect of artificial
light—is treated boldly, vigorously, not always very
subtly), and the marvellously painter-like plates of
Marriage à la Mode, so much more pictorial than the

brilliant line-engravings executed much earlier after those subjects. But not, be it observed, mentioned by Challoner Smith amongst the Earloms, are two other prints in which, in the reproduction of still-life, engraving in mezzotint reaches high-water mark : I mean the now most justly sought-for plates after the Fruit and Flower Pieces of Van Huysum. By James Watson, a contemporary of Earlom's, more or less, about a hundred and sixty prints are described. By J. R. Smith—who engraved so many of the finest of the Sir Joshuas—there are described two hundred, but by the John Smith who, a century earlier, recorded almost innumerable Knellers, there are all but three hundred. The difference in the number of plates produced by the younger men and by the elder—James Watson, Earlom, and J. R. Smith upon the one hand ; John Smith and Faber on the other—finds its explanation in the tendency of mezzotint to become more elaborate, more refined, more perfect, presumably slower, during the hundred years or so that separated the beginning, not from the end indeed (for the end, strictly speaking, is not yet), but from the very crown and crest of the achievement. Much of the early work is very vigorous. John Smith, especially, was within limited lines a sterling artist ; though mainly, like the portrait painters that he worked after, without obvious attractiveness and indeed without subtlety. The exceedingly rare examples of Ludwig von Siegen and of Prince Rupert show that these men—at the very beginning even—were artists and not bunglers. But when one compares that early work, John Smith's even—done, all of it, when the art was but in its robust childhood —with the infinitely more refined and flexible performance of the men of the Eighteenth Century, one wonders only at the great body of achievement, dexterous, delicate, faultlessly graceful, vouchsafed to the practitioners of mezzotint during the last decades of that later epoch. And between the distinctly later work and the distinctly earlier, of the less engaging executants, there came, be it remembered, the masculine art of M'Ardell, a link in the chain; for M'Ardell learnt something from the early men, and was the master of more than one of the more recent. He is admirable especially in his rendering of the portraits of men.

A vast proportion of the work of the first practitioners of Mezzotint appeals rather to the collector of portraits for likeness' sake, than to the collector of prints for beauty's sake and Art's. Such a collector is a specialist the nature of whose specialty obliges him to amass a certain amount of artistic production without necessarily having any great regard for the Art that is in it. We are not concerned, in this volume, with his specialty, honourable and serviceable as it may be—a book which, by reason of more pressing claims, leaves out of consideration the manly and yet highly refined labours of Nanteuil, Edelinck, the Drevets (masters of reproductive work in pure "line"), may well be pardoned if it does not pause over mere portraiture—I mean, the less artistic portraiture—in mezzotint. The collector who is as yet but a beginner should be encouraged to direct his eye to the more statedly and purposely artistic—to the hill-tops where he will find already, as his comrades in research, those who have brought to the task of collecting a long experience and a chastened taste. In other words, the generation of Reynolds and of Gainsborough, or else the generation of Romney and of Morland, has to be reached before the mezzotint collector can lay hands on the great prizes of his pursuit. The perfectly translated art of these painters is amongst the few things which may be accounted popular and yet may be accounted noble.

In saying this, I do not preclude myself from saying also that I think the sums given at present for the most favourite instances of mezzotint engraving are distinctly excessive. We will look at a few of them in detail, on a later page. Fashion knows little reasonableness—but little moderation—and hence it is that a translation of Reynolds, gracious and engaging, commands, if it happens to be at all rare, the price, and often more than the price, of an original and important creation of Dürer's, or even of Rembrandt's. But what shall we say when we have to recollect that, at the present moment, even the mezzotints after Hoppner are ridiculously dear!

Of all the masters of the Eighteenth or early Nineteenth Century, it is Sir Joshua Reynolds who has been engraved most amply. It is safe to say that there are something like four hundred prints after

his painted work—prints of the great time, I mean,
ending not later than 1820, and taking, amongst
others, no account of the smaller plates of which S.
W. Reynolds executed so many. The latest and best
Catalogue of these great Reynolds prints is that of
Dr. Hamilton—a labour of diligence and loving care
undertaken in our own generation. Of the painters
of the British School, Morland probably comes next
to Reynolds, in respect of the number of engravings
executed after his work. Apart from prints in stipple,
there exist after Morland something like two hundred
mezzotints. A systematic Catalogue, with states and
all, is still to be desired, as a sure practical guide to
the collector of Morland; but meanwhile useful service
has certainly been rendered by the Exhibitions at the
Messrs. Vokins's, for these were wonderfully comprehensive, and with them careful lists — only just
short of being catalogues *raisonnés*—have been issued.
William Ward—Morland's brother-in-law—and J. R.
Smith, with whom he was associated, were his two
principal engravers; but many another accomplished
craftsman had a hand in popularising his labours by
reproducing his themes—amongst them John Young,
the author of the rare and little known, and poetic
plate, *Travellers.* Mr. Percy Horne—himself, like Dr.
Hamilton, a well-known collector—has done for Gainsborough and Romney what Dr. Hamilton has done
for Sir Joshua. In one volume, charmingly illustrated
with a few specimen subjects, Mr. Percy Horne has
issued a Catalogue of the engraved portraits and fancy

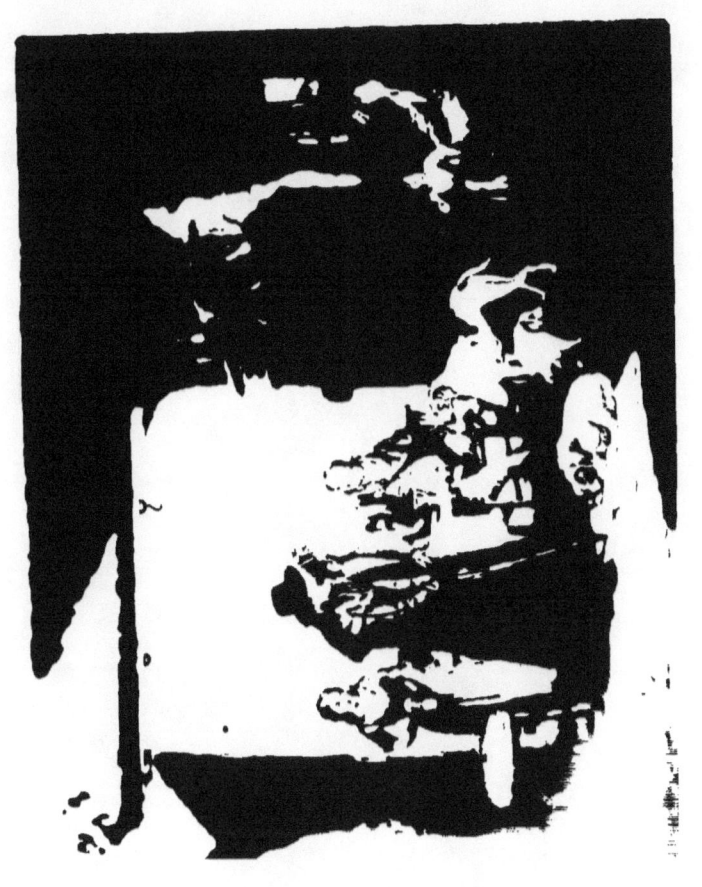

subjects painted by Gainsborough and by Romney—
the Gainsborough pieces of which he has taken note
having been published between 1760 and 1820; the
Romneys, between 1770 and 1830. By Gainsborough,
there are eighty-eight, of which seventy-seven are portraits. The numbers include some in stipple and a few
even in line, but the bulk are, of course, mezzotints.
By Romney—somehow more popular with the engravers, and, it would seem, with the public—there
are no less than a hundred and forty-five, of which a
hundred and thirty-six are portraits. But it is difficult, in this matter, to draw the line very sharply,
owing to the habit of the beauties of that day to be
painted not only as themselves, but "as Miranda,"
"as Sensibility," and the like. Mr. Horne himself reminds us, by cross references in his index, that even
of the few Romneys which he has chosen to catalogue as "fancy subjects," some are in truth portraits.
Among the engraved Romney portraits, no less than
twenty are avowed representations of the fascinating
woman who inspired Romney as did no other soul,
and without whose presence he not seldom pined.
She came to him first as Emma Hart, or Emma Lyon,
mistress of Charles Greville. He knew her afterwards
as the wife of Sir William Hamilton. The modified
and unforbidding Classicism of her beauty accorded
well with his ideal—helped perhaps to form it—and,
admirable as is much of the work of his in which she
had no place, Romney is most completely Romney
when it is Lady Hamilton he is recording.

The value of an average Romney print is to-day at least as high as that of an average Reynolds, and much higher than that of an average Gainsborough. An exceptional print like his *Mrs. Carwardine*, than which nothing is finer—a well-built gentlewoman, seen in profile, in close white cap, her head bent prettily over a nestling child, and her arms clasped at his back—sells for about a hundred guineas, and, in a fine impression, is scarcely likely to fetch less. It was engraved by J. R. Smith in 1781. Very beautiful and delicate, though not perhaps so extremely rare, is the *Elizabeth, Countess of Derby*, engraved by John Dean. Two hundred pounds has been fetched by Raphael Smith's engraving of Romney's Lady Warwick. Of Gainsboroughs, perhaps the very finest is one engraved by Dean; this is the *Mrs. Elliot*, a print of 1779; a very great rarity; a thing of delightful and dignified beauty, and in its exquisite delicacy, quite as characteristic of the engraver as of the original artist. It is a long time since any impression has been sold. About £70 was the last chronicled price for it. It would fetch more, so experts think, did it reappear to-day.

The highest price ever yet paid for a print after Sir Joshua is, as I am told, £350; and this was given for an impression of Thomas Watson's print after the picture sometimes called "An Offering to Hymen"— the *Hon. Mrs. Beresford, with the Marchioness Townshend and the Hon. Mrs. Gardiner*. For a while, the *Ladies Waldegrave*, engraved by Valentine Green, was considered at the top of the tree. £270 has been cheerfully paid for it. Mr. Urban Noseda — than whom no dealer in England is a greater specialist in mezzotint, for he has inherited, it seems, his mother's eye — the eye which made that lady so desirable a friend to the collector, a quarter of a century ago — Mr. Urban Noseda (if I can get somehow to the end of a sentence so involved and awkward that I am beginning to feel it must necessarily be very clever too) tells me, from Notes to which he has had access, that the original price of even the most important of these Sir Joshua prints was never more than a guinea and a half, and that not a few were issued at five shillings.

The Morland prices still seem moderate when compared with those of average Sir Joshuas: actually cheap when compared with those that are finest and rarest. Lately, the charming pair, *A Visit to the Child at Nurse* and *A Visit to the Child at School*, fetched, at Sotheby's, twenty-seven guineas; the *Farmer's Stable* fetched, at the Huth Sale, £11, 10s.; the *Carrier's Stable*, not long since at Christie's, fetched twenty-one guineas; *Fisherman going out*, by S. W. Reynolds, has realised £17; *The Story of Letitia*, a small set, has realised £30, but would to-day fetch more — in fine condition. Mr. Noseda says — and I suppose those other great authorities on mezzotint, Messrs. Colnaghi, would confirm him — that the original prices of the Morlands ranged from seven and sixpence to a guinea. Great as the difference is between the sum first asked and the sum now obtained, I cannot, in the case of this so genial, graceful, acceptable, observant master, think it is excessive. A generation that has gone a little mad over J. F. Millet and other interesting French rustic painters, may allow itself some healthy enthusiasm when George Morland is to the front.

CHAPTER XII

*Lithography, the convenient invention of Senefelder
—Its recent Revival due to the French and Whistler—
Fantin—Whistler's Lithographs only inferior to his
Etchings—C. H. Shannon's Lithographs the best ex-
pression of his art—Lithography and Etching compared
—Will Rothenstein—The Lithographs of Roussel—
Other Draughtsmen on Stone or Transfer-Paper—
The Modern Lithograph foolishly costly.*

A FINAL chapter I devote to another of the most justi-
fiable and reasonable of the more recent fads in Print
Collecting—to a branch of the collector's pursuit far
less important, indeed, and far less interesting than
Etching, far less historic than Mezzotint, but far more
creditable than the mania of the inartistic for the
pretty ineptitude of the coloured print. I am speaking of Lithography.

Men who are familiar with the later development of
artistic work, know that not exactly alongside of the
very real and admirable Revival of Etching, but closely
following behind it, there has proceeded some renewal
of interest in the art of drawing upon stone, which, in
1796, was invented by Senefelder. Often, however,
nowadays, it is not literally "on stone." Without
defending the change—and yet without the possibility
of violently accusing it, seeing the achievements which

at least it has not forbidden—I may note that, as a matter of fact, a transfer-paper, and not the prepared stone, is, very frequently in our day, the substance actually drawn on.

Well, the renewal of interest in the art of Lithography owes something to the Frenchmen of the present generation, and something too to Mr. Whistler. I say "the present generation" in talking of the French, because (not to speak of the qualities obtained two generations ago by our English Prout), Gavarni's "velvety quality" and the "fever and freedom of Daumier" were noticeable and might have been influential before the days of our present young men. The work of Fantin-Latour, one may take it, has been to them an example, and, yet later, the work of Whistler. Fantin-Latour—that delightful painter of flowers and of the poetic nude—has endowed us in Lithography as well, with reveries of the nude, or of the slightly robed. They are all done in freely scraped crayon. A few of them—such as *The Genius of Music*, or the quite recent *To Stendhal*—the collector of the lithograph should certainly possess. But I must turn, in detail, to Mr. Whistler.

Mr. Tom Way, who knows as much about Lithography as any one — and more, perhaps, than any one about the lithographs of Whistler — assured me, a year since, that something like a hundred drawings on the stone, or transfer-paper (for Mr. Whistler sometimes uses the one and sometimes the other), had been wrought by one whose reputation is secure as the master-etcher of our time. Since then Mr. Way has accurately and eulogistically catalogued them. They amount now, or did when Mr. Way finished his catalogue, to exactly a hundred and thirty. But Mr. Whistler is always working. Let us recall a few of them—and most, though indeed by no means all, of them have been seen in an exhibition held scarcely a year ago in the rooms of the Fine Art Society. Before then, they were wont to be shown privately by one or two dealers. Earlier still, they were not shown at all, though a few of the finest of them had been long ago wrought. There was that most distinguished drawing that was published for a penny in the *Whirlwind*—the lady seated, with a hat on, and one arm pendant. It is called *The Winged Hat*. As in Mr. Whistler's rare little etching of the slightly-draped cross-kneed girl stooping over a baby, one enjoys, in *The Winged Hat*, the suggestion of delicate tone on the whole surface: the working of the face is particularly noteworthy by reason of the subtle way in which the draughtsman had suggested, by means of the handling of his chalk, a different texture. "By means of the handling of his chalk," did I write?—perhaps a little too confidently. One can't quite say how he did really get it. But he has got it, somehow.

Then there is that admirable portfolio, of only six or so, the Goupils published—containing the *Limehouse*, mysterious and weird, and a *Nocturne, Battersea*, wholly exquisite. Again, there is the *Battersea Bridge*, of

1878, which, good though it is, does not stand comparison with Mr. Whistler's etchings of the same and similar themes. Then there is the rare subject which people learned in Lithography are wont to account almost if not quite the Whistlerian masterpiece in the method—a drawing tenderly washed: a thing of masses and broad spaces, more than narrow lines. It is called *Early Morning*, and is a vision of the River at Battersea. It is faint—faint—of gradations the most delicate, of contrasts the least striking—a gleam of silver and white.

Later, among many others, there have been that drawing of a draped model seated which appeared in M. Marty's "L'Estampe Originale;" the *fin* portrait of M. Mallarmé—a writer so difficult to understand that by the faithful and by the outsider his profundity is taken for granted—the interesting and clever print, *The Doctor*, which adorns the "Pageant;" the *Belle Dame paresseuse*, with, most especially it may be, the quality of a chalk drawing; the *Belle Jardinière*, which has something, but by no means all of the infinite freedom of the etching of *The Garden*; again, *The Balcony* with people peering down from it, as if at a procession—and procession indeed it was, since the thing was wrought on the day of Carnot's funeral. Then, in the *Forge* and *The Smith of the Place du Dragon* there is the tender soft grey quality which people learned in these things conceive, I think generally, to be impossible to "transfer."

But of the younger artists who have worked in

224

Lithography it is time to say something. Mr. Frank
Short, with his placid dream of *Putney*, with the
intricate rhythm of line of his *Timber-Ships, Yarmouth*,
should not be passed by. Nor Mr. Francis Bate, who,
to draw as he has drawn, and see as he has seen, *The
Whiting Mill*, could not possibly have been wanting in
originality of expression or of sight. Nor Mr. George
Clausen, again, whose *Hay Barn* bears witness not only
to his easy command of *technique*, but to his flexibility.
It is one of those treatments of rustic life in which
Mr. Clausen has been wont to show the influence of
Millet, if not of Bastien Lepage. It is of a realism
artistically subdued, yet undeniable. Of the work of
C. H. Shannon I must speak a good deal more fully, for
of C. H. Shannon, Lithography is the particular art.
He is no beginner at Lithography: no maker of first
experiments. I do not know that he—like Mr. Short
—is an engraver in any way. He is not, like Mr.
Whistler, celebrated on two continents as etcher and
painter to boot. He is above all things draughtsman
—draughtsman poetic and subtle. The air of Lithography he breathes as his native air.

C. H. Shannon's art it is by no means easy for the
healthy normal person to appreciate at once. It is
possible even for a student of the matter to lose
sight of Shannon's poetry and sensitiveness, in a fit of
impatience because the anatomy of his figures does
not always seem to be true, or because his sentiment
has not robustness. I have a lurking suspicion that I
was myself rather slow to appreciate him. Few people's

appreciation of the original in Art, comes to them all at once. And touchy folk—unreasonable, almost irresponsible—are apt to blame one on this account. One has "swallowed one's words," they say—because one has modified an opinion. The world, even the intelligent world, they querulously grumble, was not ready to receive them. Is that so very amazing? Themselves, doubtless, were born with every faculty matured—they possessed, upon their mother's breasts, a nice discrimination of the virtues of Lafitte of '69. Some of us, under such circumstances, can but crave their tolerance—we were born duller.

Of lithographic *technique*, Mr. C. H. Shannon—to go back to him, after an inexcusable digression—is a master; and here let it be said that not only does he draw upon the stone invariably, whilst Mr. Whistler (it has been named before) sometimes does and sometimes does not draw on it, but he insists also upon printing his own impressions. He has a press; he is an enthusiast; he sees the thing through. The precise number of his lithographs it is not important to know. What is important, is to insist upon the relative "considerableness" of nearly all of them. With him the thoroughly considered composition takes the place of the dainty sketch. Faulty the works of Charles Shannon may be, in certain points; deficient in certain points; but rarely indeed are they slight, either in conception or execution. Of each one of them may it be said that it is a serious work: the seriousness as apparent in the more or less realistic treatment of *The Modeller* as in *Delia*, ideal and opulent and Titianesque. The *Ministrants*, of 1894, is perhaps his most important. What is more exquisite than the just suggested movements of *The Sisters?* *Sea-Breezes* is noteworthy, of course, in composition, and refined, of course, in effect.

Before I go on to discuss a few others of the modern men, it may be more interesting to remind the reader— it may be, even to inform him—what is and what may hope to be Lithography's place. In such signs of its revival as are now apparent, he will surely rejoice. One does rejoice to find an artist equipped with some new medium of expression—some medium of expression, at all events, by which his work, while remaining auto- graphic, may yet be widely diffused. And the art or craft of Lithography, whatever it does not do, does at least enable the expert in it to produce and scatter broadcast, by the hundred or the thousand if he choose, work which shall have all or nearly all the quality of a pencil or chalk drawing, or, if it is desired, much of the quality even of a drawing that is washed. This is excellent; and then again there is the com- mercial advantage of relatively rapid and quite inex- pensive printing. But what the serious and impartial amateur and collector of Fine Art will have to notice on the other side, is, first of all, that Lithography is not richly endowed with a separate quality of its own. With work that is printed from a metal plate, this is quite otherwise. Mezzotint has a charm that is its own, entirely. And Line-Engraving has the particular charm of Line-Engraving. And Etching—the biting, which gives vigour now, and now extreme delicacy; the printing, which deliberately enhances this or modifies that; the burr, the dry-point work, its intended effect; the papers, and the different results they yield, of tone or luminousness—all these things contribute to, and are a part of, Etching's especial quality and especial delight.

A comparison between Lithography and Etching in particular — putting other mediums aside — leads to further reflections. Lithography lacks the relief of etched work. " You can't have grey and black lines " —a skilled etcher says to me, who enjoys Lithography as well as Etching, and sometimes practises it—" you can't have grey and black lines, in that the printing of a lithograph is surface-printing, and every mark upon the stone prints equally black. Therefore for grey work in Lithography, you must have a grain upon the stone—or on the transfer-paper—that your drawing is made on." And he adds, " Whatever can be done upon a lithographic stone, can be done with a much higher quality upon a plate." And the soft grey line, he says, when got upon the stone—" well, if that is what you want, in a soft-ground etching it can be got much better."

As to Mezzotint again, to compare the quality of a fine mezzotint from copper, with any quality that is obtainable in stone, would, generally, be absurd. We are brought back, however, to that which is Lithography's especial virtue and convenience—it gives the autographic quality of the pencil drawing, of the chalk drawing, of the drawing that is washed.

When, in these last words, I tried to indicate Lithography's natural limits, and said, practically, that its main function was to produce "battalions" where ordinary drawing must produce but "single spies," I said nothing that need encourage readers to suppose that its process lay perfectly at the command of every draughtsman, and that the first-comer, did he know well how to draw, would get from the lithographic stone every quality the stone could yield. And this being so, it can surprise no one if in a chapter on the Revival of Lithography I give conspicuous place to the young men who have really fagged at it, rather than to the possibly more accomplished, the certainly more famous artists who have drawn just lately on the tracing-paper, oftener than not in complimentary recognition of the fact that now a hundred years have passed since Alois Senefelder invented the method which, half a century later, Hulmandel did something to perfect.

Mr. C. H. Shannon—pre-eminently noticeable among these younger men—has been discussed already. We will look now at the work of another of them—Mr. Will Rothenstein, whose mind, whose hand-work, is conspicuously unlike Mr. Shannon's, in that, though he can be romantic, he can scarcely be poetic. A vivid realism is his characteristic, and, with that vivid realism, romance, phantasy, caprice—either or all—may find themselves in company; but poetry, hardly. Mr. Rothenstein—as there is some reason, perhaps, for telling the collector—is not only young, but extremely young. His series of Oxford lithographs were wrought, most of them, when he was between twenty and two-and-twenty years old. It was an audacious adventure, with youth for its excuse. For this set of Oxford portraits was to be the abstract of the Oxford of a day. In it, Professors and Heads of Houses are—men who for perhaps a generation remain in their place—but in it, too, are athletes, engaging undergraduates, lads whose achievements may become a tradition, but whose places know them no more. The first part of the "Oxford Characters"—that is the proper name of it—appeared in June 1893. In it, is the portrait of that great Christ Church boating man, W. L. Fletcher, and a portrait of Sir Henry Acland, for which another more august-looking rendering of the same head and figure was after a while substituted. Again, there is an admirable vision of Max Müller—Mr. Rothenstein's high-water mark, perhaps, in that which he might probably suppose to be the humble art of likeness-taking.

Quite outside the charmed Oxford life are the subjects of some of Mr. Rothenstein's generally piquant portraits. There is the portrait of Emile Zola, for instance. I never saw the man. This may or may not be a *terre-à-terre* view of him. Most probably it is. But certainly the face, with its set lips and hollow cheeks, is cleverly rendered, though in such rendering we may fancy not so much the author of the *Faute de l'Abbé Mouret* and of the *Page d'Amour*, as the author of *Nana* and of *Le Ventre de Paris*. Again, there is a portrait, at once refined and forcible, of that great gentleman, path-breaking novelist, and dainty connoisseur, Edmond de Goncourt, elderly, but with fires unquenched in the dark, piercing eyes, and the great decoration, so to say, of snow-white hair. Then again, the pretty, pleasing lady, the fresh young thing with her big bonnet—the lady seen full-face, her lips drawn so tenderly. Such flesh and blood as hers, had the Millament of Congreve. If sometimes in them the anatomy of the figures is expressed insufficiently, these works are at least executed with well-acquired knowledge of the effects to which Lithography best lends itself. It can escape no one that, whatever be their faults, the artist utters in them a note that is his own.

To trace, with fairness, the revival of Lithography, even in England only, it should be mentioned that a generation after the achievements of Samuel Prout—his records of architecture in Flanders and in Germany—and the somewhat overrated performances of Harding, the members of the Hogarth Sketching Club made one night, at the house of Mr. Way, the elder—the date was the 15th of December, 1874—a set of drawings on the stone. They must be rare, now. Indeed the only copy I have seen was that shown to me at the printing-house in Wellington Street. One of the best was Charles Green's drawing of two men—ostlers, both of them, or of ostler rank—one of them lighting his pipe. The hand is excellently modelled : the light and shade of the whole subject has crispness and vigour. Sir James Linton contributed a *Coriolanus* subject, in something more than outline, though not fully expressed—and yet it is beautifully drawn. Mr. Coke sent a *Massacre of the Innocents*, classic and charming in contour; while to look at the *Sir Galahad* of Mr. E. J. Gregory is to recall to mind completely the great Romantic Gregory of that early day.

In the Paris Exhibition of Lithographs and in that at Mr. Dunthorne's, there have figured a group of subjects done lately by well-known Academicians and others, and printed—some of them with novel effects —by or under the close direction of Mr. Goulding, that famous printer of etchings, who now, it seems, has the laudable ambition of rivalling, as a printer of lithographs, the great house of Way. He has his own methods. The original work is of extremely various quality. Much of it was produced somewhat hurriedly. I do not mean that the drawings were done rapidly, or that it would have been wrong if they had been; for, obviously, the rapid drawing of the capable is often as fine as the slowest, and has the interest of a more urgent message. I mean that they were done, for the most part, by those not versed, as yet, in such secrets as Lithography possesses. Yet, coming often from artists of distinction, many of them have merits. Not much is finer than a girl's head, by Mr. Watts. It is mostly "in tone;" and it is scarcely too much to say of it that it is strong as anything of Leonardo's— as anything of Holbein's, one might as easily declare, did not Holbein's name suggest, along with strength, a certain austerity which Mr. Watts mostly avoids. There is a graceful figure-drawing by Lord Leighton, who was interested in the new movement, but who was far too sensible to set vast store by what—as I remember that he wrote to tell me—was the only lithographic drawing he had ever executed. There are strong studies by Sargent—rather brutal perhaps in light and shade—of male models, whose partial nudity there is little to render interesting.

We are brought back then to the work of artists not Academicians at all—men some of them comparatively young in years, but older in a faithful following of the lines on which the craft of Lithography most properly moves. There is Mr. C. J. Watson, for instance. The personal note—which, I cannot conceal it, I esteem most of all, and most of all must revel in—the personal note may be, with him, a little wanting; but thorough craftsman he undeniably is. And by Mr. Oliver Hall, one of the most delightful of our younger etchers, who as an etcher has been treated in his place, there is a vision of some grey sweeping valley— *Wensleydale*—with trees only in middle distance, or in the remote background. In it, and perhaps even more especially in that quite admirable lithograph, *The Edge of the Moor*, we recognise that way of looking at the world which we know in the etchings; but the intelligence and sensitiveness of the artist have suffered him, or led him rather, to modify the work: to properly adapt it to the newer medium. *The Edge of the Moor* is, I have implied, quite masterly; and then again there is a tree-study in which Mr. Hall recalls those broad and massive, yet always elegant sketches made by the great Cotman, in the latest years, generally, of a life not too prolonged.

Again, among fine lithographs exhibited or not exhibited, there is, by Mr. Raven Hill, *The Oyster-Barrow*—a marvellously vivid, faithful study of " Over the Water " (or of Dean's Yard, it may be) by night —and the equally momentary, spontaneous vision of *The Baby*, with the rotundity of Boucher, and more than the expressiveness of the late Italian : a baby lost, one must avow, to all angelic dreams, and set on carnal things. Perhaps Mr. George Thomson's finest lithograph remains the *Brentford Eyot*, though there is charm of movement in at least one figure-study. By Mr. Charles Sainton there is a luxurious head of just the type one might expect from the author of silverpoints promptly seductive and popular. Mr. Walter Sickert's work, whether you like it or not, at least has, visibly, its source in personal observation and deliberate principle.

By M. Théodore Roussel there are a whole group of lithographs, dainty and delightful, exquisite and fresh —with so much of his own in them, as well as something, of course, of Mr. Whistler's. By the side of his *Scene on the River*—a quaint Battersea or Chelsea bit, I take it—place one of his supple nudities, and against his supple nudity place his *Opera Cloak*. The man is a born artist—he not only draws but sees, sees with refinement and distinction. And there must come a time when Roussel's work will be appreciated far more widely.

By Mr. Jacomb Hood there is a spirited elderly man's portrait, and an *Idyll*—a Classical or an Arcadian *pas de quatre*—of singular, unwonted charm. By Mr. Corbett, the semi-classical landscape painter, there is a nude study—a torso, magnificently modelled. By Mr. Solomon Solomon there is a *Venus*, correct in draughtsmanship of course; nor wanting in dramatic quality, for it is not the undressed woman of too many students, but Aphrodite herself—"Vénus, à sa proie attachée." And lastly—since I cannot merely catalogue—there is Mr. Anning Bell, who has bestowed on us enjoyable designs—book-plates *hors ligne* indeed, so charming are they in their reticence and grace and measured beauty. In Lithography, we may be thankful for the Tanagra-like grace of his *Dancing Girl*. But "Why Tanagra?" am I asked. Because Classical without austerity: provokingly Modern, and yet endowed with the legitimate and endless fascination of Style.

And now, to end with, it seems advisable to say something on the very practical matter of the acquisition of lithographs by the collector, and on their cost. The money value of the lithograph is most uncertain. When the lithograph appears in a popular magazine —the actual lithograph, remember; no merely photographic reproduction of it—it is, on publication, valued at a couple of shillings, or at a shilling, or, as in the extraordinary case of publication in the extinct *Whirl-wind*, even at a penny. The prices I have named are, most of them at least, absurd; but on the other hand the dealer's price—sometimes the original artist's price—for an impression, is wont to be excessive. A lithograph can be printed—as magazine issue suffices to show—in considerable numbers. Nothing restricts it as the ordinary unsteeled etching is restricted: still less, as the dry-point is restricted. There is no reason, except the scantiness of the public demand, why it should not be issued in an edition almost as large as that of the average book. Nor is the printing costly. Nor has the drawing on stone or transfer-paper involved anything more of labour, skill, or genius, than is involved in the preparation of a single chapter of a fine novel—of a single paragraph in a fine short story. Yet while the novel sells probably at six shillings, and the whole short story (and other short stories along with it) sells, very likely, at three-and-sixpence, the impression of a lithograph—unless, as I have said before, it be published in a magazine—is sold seldom for less than a guinea. The Fine Art Society asked something like three guineas apiece, I think, for the lithographs of Mr. Whistler, when it exhibited them. I mentioned the circumstance to a man who was interested in the question, both as artist and connoisseur. "You do not want to vulgarise lithographs," he said, "by issuing too many impressions." I wonder how many impressions of Gray's "Elegy" have been issued? And how many of the "Ode to Duty?" And I wonder whether Wordsworth and Gray have been "vulgarised," because the fruit of their genius has been widely diffused?

About five shillings seems a reasonable price for a lithograph issued in our time. When draughtsmen (and their publishers) realise this, they will confer a boon upon themselves, and will do no injury whatever to us who admire them. And until they do realise it, the collecting of lithographs will go on only within a limited circle—a circle of rich people, possibly, but most likely idle, and therefore probably, at bottom, unappreciative. Indeed such a circle cannot be said to consist, truly, of "collectors." They will be "purchasers," rather—which is a different affair.

APPENDIX

CERTAIN WOODCUTS

Though when this volume was first planned, it was supposed that in its regular course it might embrace a chapter upon Woodcuts, mature consideration and the progress of the work revealed to me the undesirableness of treating either by my own or by a more qualified hand the theme of Woodcuts, at any important length ; and in adding here a Note on certain examples of that ancient art, it is convenient that I should say plainly why the matter is left to an Appendix.

First, then, treatment exhaustive, or adequate, could only have been supplied by some one other than myself : my own knowledge of Woodcuts being merely that of an outsider who cannot withhold a measure of interest from any department of Art. To have invited the continued presence of an expert—an enthusiast in the particular thing would have been at least to deprive the book of that unity of sentiment which comes of undivided authorship, and which even in a work of this sort may conceivably be a benefit : moreover, although a complete Guide to Old Prints must include of necessity many words about woodcuts, it was doubtful whether the subject of " Fine Prints " involved even a mention of them. I mean, it might be argued, plausibly, that woodcuts, however fine in their design and the design of the giant Dürer was given to some of them—are in the very nature of things scarcely " fine " in execution. To say that the best recall the utterance of noble sentiment by rough and uncouth tongue, is not for a moment to minimise their sterling worth. Lastly, too, the collectors of them—in England at least—are scanty in the extreme. When—one may ask —do they appear at Sotheby's? As objects of research, they seem hopelessly out of fashion. It may be that they had their day when only the Past was thought interesting. But it has been one of the objects of this book to acknowledge specially the interest of more modern achievement, and not to call contemporary genius only "talent," until it is contemporary no longer, and, being dead—and dead long since—may be accorded its due.

But I should like to tell the beginner in the study of prints one or two quite elementary things—as, for instance, that the best and the most numerous of old woodcuts are German; that not a few of the earlier masters of copperplate engraving carried out upon the wood-block certain of their designs; that in the days of Bewick the art had a certain revival, finding itself well adapted—in book illustration at all events—to the rendering of Bewick's homely and rustic themes. And so one might go on—but after all, book illustration is no part of one's theme. Let it just be mentioned about Bewick—before we leave the English woodcuts for the earlier masters—that the rarest and in some respects the most important of his works (not, I think, the most fascinating) is the piece known as the *Chillingham Bull*. When only a few impressions had been taken from it, the original block split. Hence the print's scarcity; and in its scarcity we see in part at least the cause of its attractiveness.

A passage in the last annual report made by Mr. Sidney Colvin to the Trustees of the British Museum—in his capacity as Keeper of the Prints—reminds me of a splendid gift made lately to the nation by the munificence of Mr. William Mitchell: a gift which the possession of money alone, and of a generous intention, could not have

242

empowered him to make; only deep knowledge, and real diligence in the art of collecting, made the thing possible. Through Mr. Mitchell's gift there passes into the store-house of the Department of Prints this connoisseur's collection of German and other woodcuts, including a series of those by Albert Dürer, which is almost complete, and "quite unrivalled," Mr. Colvin says, "in quality and condition." The whole array includes 1290 early woodcuts, chiefly, as will be seen, German, and constituted for the most part as follows :—104 by anonymous German artists of the fifteenth and sixteenth centuries; 151 single cuts by Albert Dürer, together with the Little Passion (set of proofs), the Life of the Virgin (first state, without text), and the Great Passion, the Life of the Virgin, and the Apocalypse (all with Latin text, edition of 1511); 63 by Hans Schaufelein, including two sets of proofs of two series of the Passion; 18 by Hans Springinklee, including 14 proofs of illustrations to "Hortulus Animae ;" 7 by Wolfgang Huber ; 36 by Hans Baldung ; 7 by Johann Wechtlin ; 19 by Hans Sebald Beham ; 43 by Lucas Cranach, including an unique impression of the St. George, printed in gold on a blue ground; 60 by Albert Altdorfer ; 40 by Hans Burgkmair; 313 by or attributed to Hans Holbein ; 9 by Urs Graf; 12 by Heinrich Holzmüller ; 14 by J. von Calcar; 5 by Jost Amman ; 11 by Anton von Worms; 16 by Lucas van Leyden ; 6 attributed to Geoffroy Troy; one attributed to Marie de Medicis: the large view of Venice by Jacopo de Barbarj, first state ; 9 by Niccolò Boldrini ; 5 by I.B. with the bird.

An inspection of this collection alone, in the Museum Print Room, constitutes, at first hand, an introduction to the study of an ancient, quaint, and pregnant art.

So much had I written when there came to me a note from Mr. O. Gutekunst, curiously confirming, on the whole, the view that I had taken as to the small place filled by

Woodcuts, generally, in the scheme of the modern collector. It is not, however, so much on this account that I
print the note here, as because it contains one or two
particulars—especially as to money value—not named
by me, and which may be of interest. "The history of
Woodcuts," says Mr. O. Gutekunst—instructing my ignorance—"begins, as you know, practically with printed
books in which the woodcuts took the place of the minia-
tures, &c., in Manuscripts. During almost the whole of the
Fifteenth Century the Woodcut was thus confined to illustration, and belongs far more to the bibliophile than to the
Print-collector. *Vide ' Biblia Pauperum'* and similar works
—in Italy, Germany, and the Netherlands—Block Books,
Incunabula, &c., &c. The great period of Wood Engraving as a distinct art by itself—a then and now appreciated
mode of expression of the artist—is the first half of the
Sixteenth Century." Mr. Gutekunst then cites to me works
by masters, some of whom have been named. "There were
Dürer, Cranach, Holbein, Altdorfer, Brosamer," he says.
"Fine specimens of these men's work, particularly portraits, and when printed in one, two, or more colours, are
now, and always must have been, exceedingly rare, with
prices varying from, say £20 to £80 for single very fine
specimens. The decadence begins with Jost Amman,
for instance, in Germany, and Andreani, say, in Italy,
where the works of earlier, and more particularly the
masters of the wrong half of the Sixteenth Century, were
reproduced in chiar-oscuro.". With the exception perhaps
of the remarkable impressions in Mr. Mitchell's collection,
Mr. O. Gutekunst asserts that the finest specimens always
were most appreciated in Germany, and adds, "There
has ever been more interest taken in Woodcuts by German
collectors than by any others."

BIBLIOGRAPHY

ALVIN, LOUIS. Catalogue Raisonné de l'Œuvre des trois frères, Jean, Jerome, et Antoine Wierix. 8vo. 1866.

ANDRESEN, ANDREAS. Der Deutsche Peintre-Graveur, oder die Deutschen Maler als Kupferstichsammler. Two vols. 1864–73.

APELL, ALOYS. Handbuch für Kupferstichsammler. 1880.

AUMÜLLER, E. Les Petits Maîtres Allemands. Barthel et Sebald Beham. 8vo. 1881.

—— Les Petits Maîtres Allemands. Jacques Binck. 8vo. 1893.

BARTSCH, ADAM. Le Peintre-Graveur, and Supplement. 22 vols. 1803–43.

BÉRALDI, HENRI. Les Graveurs du Dix-Neuvième Siècle. 4to.

BLANC, CHARLES. L'Œuvre Complet de Rembrandt. Two vols. 8vo.

BOCHER, EMMANUEL. Les Gravures Françaises du Dix-Huitième Siècle. Six volumes at present, viz. :—
    Nicholas Lavreince. 1875.
    Pierre Antoine Baudouin. 1875.
    Jean Baptiste Siméon Chardin. 1876.
    Nicolas Lancret. 1877.
    Augustin de St. Aubin. 1879.
    Jean Michel Moreau, le jeune. 1882.

BOURCARD, GUSTAVE. Les Estampes du Dix-Huitième Siècle. 1885.

BRYAN, MICHAEL. Dictionary of Painters and Engravers. 8vo. 1865.

Supplement, by Ottley. 8vo. 1886.

A New Edition, by Graves. 8vo. 1884–86.

CHAVIGNERIE, EMILE BELLIER de la, et LOUIS AUVRAY. Dictionnaire Général des Artistes de l'École Française. Two vols. 1885.

COHEN, HENRI. Guide de l'Amateur des Livres à Vignette, du XVIIIᵐᵉ Siècle. 1873.

A New Edition. 1880.

CUMBERLAND, GEORGE. An Essay on the Utility of Collecting the Best Works of the Ancient Engravers of the Italian School. 4to. 1827.

DANIELL, FREDERICK B. Catalogue Raisonné of the Engraved Works of Richard Cosway, R.A. With a Memoir of Cosway by Sir Philip Currie. 1890.

DELABORDE, LE VICOMTE HENRI. La Gravure en Italie avant Marc Antoine. 1882.

—— Le Département des Estampes à la Bibliothèque Nationale.

DIDOT, A. FIRMIN. Histoire de Gravure sur Bois. 8vo. 1863.

—— Les Graveurs de Portrait en France. 8vo. 1875–77.

—— Les Drevet: Catalogues Raisonnés de leur Œuvre. 1876.

DOBSON, AUSTIN. Life and Works of William Hogarth. 1891.

DRAKE, Sir W. R. A Descriptive Catalogue of the Etched Work of Francis Seymour Haden. 8vo. 1880.

DUCHESNE AINÉ. Essai sur les Nielles. 8vo. 1826.

DUPLESSIS, GEORGE. De la Gravure de Portrait en France. 8vo. 1875.

BIBLIOGRAPHY

DUPLESSIS, GEORGE (and BOUCHOT). Dictionnaire des Marques et Monogrammes de Graveurs. 8vo. 1886.

DUTUIT, EUGÈNE. Manuel de l'Amateur d'Estampes. 8vo. 1881–88.

—— L'Œuvre Complet de Rembrandt. Three vols. 4to. 1883–85.

FAGAN, LOUIS. Catalogue of Woollett's Engraved Works. 8vo. 1885.

—— Catalogue of Faithorne's Engraved Works.

—— Collector's Marks. 4to. 1883.

FISHER, RICHARD. Early History of Engraving in Italy. 1886.

GILPIN, WILLIAM. An Essay on Prints. 8vo. 1781.

GONSE, LOUIS. L'Œuvre de Jules Jacquemart. 1876.

HADEN, FRANCIS SEYMOUR. About Etching. 8vo. 1878.

—— Etched Work of Rembrandt. A Monograph. 1879.

HAMERTON, PHILIP GILBERT. Etching and Etchers. 1868.
A Second Edition, revised. 1880.
A Third Edition. 1880.

HAMILTON, EDWARD. A Catalogue Raisonné of the Engraved Works of Sir Joshua Reynolds. 1874.
A Second Edition. 1880.

HORNE, HENRY PERCY. An Illustrated Catalogue of Engraved Portraits and Fancy Subjects by Gainsborough and Romney. 1891.

HYMANS, HENRI. Histoire de la Gravure dans l'École de Rubens. 8vo. 1879.

—— L'Œuvre de Lucas Vosterman. 1895.

JACKSON, JOHN. A Treatise on Wood Engraving. 8vo. 1839.
A Second Edition, enlarged. 1861.

LE BLANC. Manuel de l'Amateur d'Estampes. Two vols. 8vo. 1854.

LE BLANC. Catalogue de l'Œuvre de J. G. Wille. 8vo. 1847.

—— Catalogue de l'Œuvre de Robert Strange. 8vo. 1848.

LEHR, MAX. Wenzel von Olmütz. 1889.

—— Der Meister der Liebes Garten. 1893.

—— The Master of the Amsterdam Cabinet (Chalcographical Society). 1894.

LEYMARIE, L. DE. L'Œuvre de Gilles Demarteau l'ainé, Graveur du Roi. 1896.

LIPPMANN, F. Der Italiensche Holzschnitt. 8vo. 1885.

—— The Art of Wood Engraving in Italy in the XVth Century (English edition of the above work).

LOFTIE, Rev. W. J. A Catalogue of the Prints of Hans Sebald Beham. 1877.

MABERLY, J. The Print Collector. 1844.

MALASSIS, A. P., and THIBAUDEAU. Catalogue Raisonné de l'Œuvre Gravé et Lithographié d'Alphonse Legros. 8vo. 1877.

MARSHALL, JULIAN. Engravers of Ornament. 8vo. 1869.

MEAUME, EDOUARD. Recherches sur la Vie et les Ouvrages de Jacques Callot. Two vols. 1860.

MEYER, JULIUS. Allegemeines Kunstler Lexicon.

MIDDLETON-WAKE, Rev. C. H. Catalogue of the Etched Work of Rembrandt. 1878.

NICHOLSON, R. George Morland. 1896.

OTTLEY, W. Y. History of Engraving. Two vols. 4to. 1816.

PAPILLON, J. B. M. Traité Historique et Pratique de la Gravure en Bois. 1766.

PARTHEY, G. Hollar Catalogue. 8vo. 1858.

PASSAVANT, J. D. Le Peintre-Graveur. Six vols. 8vo. 1860–64.

PYE, JOHN, and J. L. ROGET. Notes on the " Liber Studiorum " of Turner. 8vo. 1879.

BIBLIOGRAPHY

RAWLINSON, W. G. Descriptive Catalogue of Turner's "Liber Studiorum." 8vo. 1878.

REDGRAVE, S. Dictionary of Artists of the English School. A New Edition. 1878.

ROSENBERG, ADOLF. S. and B. Beham. 1875.

ROVINSKI, DMITRI. L'Œuvre gravé de Rembrandt. Reproductions des Planches originales dans tous leurs Etats successifs. 1890.

SCOTT, WILLIAM BELL. Albert Dürer, his Life and Works. 1869.

The Little Masters.

SMITH, J. CHALLONER. British Mezzotint Portraits. Five vols. 8vo. 1878–83.

SMITH, WILLIAM. Cornelius Vischer. 8vo. 1864.

THAUSING, MORITZ. Albert Dürer. English translation. Two vols. 1882.

TIFFIN, W. B. English Mezzotint Portraits. 8vo. 1883.

WEDMORE, FREDERICK. Méryon, and Méryon's "Paris," with a Descriptive Catalogue of the Artist's Work. 8vo. 1879.

A Second Edition, revised. 8vo. 1892.

—— Whistler's Etchings: A Study and a Catalogue. 8vo. 1886.

—— Etching in England. 1895.

WILLSHIRE, W. H. An Introduction to the Study of Ancient Prints. 1874. Second Edition. Two vols. 1877.

—— Early Prints in the British Museum. Two vols. 1879–83.

WILSON, J. ("An Amateur"). A Descriptive Catalogue of the Prints of Rembrandt. 8vo. 1836.

WOLTMANN. Holbein und seine Zeit. Two vols. 1866–68.

WORNUM, R. N. Life of Holbein. 1867.

INDEX

INDEX

INDEX

252

INDEX

INDEX

255

INDEX

THE END

Printed by BALLANTYNE, HANSON & Co.
Edinburgh & London

www.ingramcontent.com/pod-product-compliance
Lightning Source LLC
Chambersburg PA
CBHW030620030726
47497CB00006B/1576